life is what you make it

LILY ROUAULT

Cover and Interior Book design by Jennifer Stimson

Edited by Carrie Jones

To Mum, thanks for always being there.

table of contents

chapter 1

Today is my final chance to achieve my dreams. My life may not be normal, but what is normal in the twenty-first century? I'm not going to let anything stand in my way, no matter what it takes. As I reach for the bar attached to my bed to swing my legs around, all I want to do is roll back into bed and hide under the duvet, but looking at my walking frame, I have to remind myself how strong I am. Eventually, I conjure up the energy to walk to the bathroom whilst holding onto the cold steel of the frame. As I try to make myself look somewhat presentable, I think about all I have accomplished over the last fourteen years of being in education. From a baby who was told that I wouldn't walk or talk, to me now with my dreams almost in sight.

"*Do we really have to go back? Why can't we start travelling early? XX*"

My best friend Jack's dream has always been to go travelling around Australia and New Zealand. He's never really been interested in going to university and getting a degree. Instead, he thinks that we achieve more by going and seeing what the world has to offer.

"Amy! Will you please get a move on! You're going to be late for your first day! I hope you're nearly ready in there." Mum's voice was becoming louder as she was getting closer and closer to the door,

Having cerebral palsy means that getting dressed can be challenging. I use a button hook to do up my shirt, which is a wire hoop on a plastic handle. I never like to ask anyone for help. I know Mum has struggled to accept this over the years and all she wants to do is make sure that I'm getting everything I need to reach my full potential. As I finish my make-up, I grab my new Ted Baker handbag that I bought on a shopping trip with Josie and Emma over the summer. I then hook it onto the edge of my frame and walk into the living room. Mum has already stood by the front door with my coat, ready to help me put it on, which always irritates me.

She packs a plastic food container in the top of my bag containing two slices of toast. She knows I never have time to eat. My doctor has told me numerous times that I shouldn't be using a handbag to lug around my heavy books as it messes with the alignment of my back. Although, the thought of wearing one of the ugly rucksacks makes me want to curl up under a rock and die.

"Are you sure you don't want me to drive you to school? I always worry about you going on those buses, and have you had your tablets?" Mum hugs me tightly. I know she always wants me to have my independence, but I will always be her baby. Unfortunately, she always holds the hug a second too long, awkward. If I want to become an actress, then I have to have as much independence as I possibly can.

"Mum, we have the same conversation every year. You know Jack always gets there early to make sure I get a seat, so please don't worry. Yes, of course, bye love you." Before she has a chance even to try and stop me again, I put on my earphones and make my way down the front path. I understand that Mum is always trying to look out for me but having my independence is so important.

I'm very much used to the neighbour's patronising looks that they have given me every day since they moved in five years ago. I even overheard one of them say to Mum once that they think she's a saint for raising a disabled child all by herself. She isn't perfect, but she's my mum, and I wouldn't have her any other way.

I get to the bus stop just as it's pulling in; I'm not quite sure how I've never missed it. Thankfully, Jack is already there waiting for me. It's so annoying how the bus driver has seen me get on this bus for the past seven years, and somehow every day, he forgets to lower the bus to pavement level.

We find a seat towards the back of the bus because we're

definitely not cool enough to sit right at the back.

"This is it! All we have to do is get through this year, then we are finally free!" Jack says whilst grinning from ear to ear like a Cheshire cat and shaking me from side to side due to his sheer excitement.

Jack and I met on the first day of year seven. I remember him coming up to me whilst being assigned our tutor groups. "Umm, excuse me, what's wrong with you? Why do you have to use a frame?"

I could tell how nervous he was even to ask. Even through, I hate this question and feel that there's nothing to say to it. Since then, he's always accepted me and supported my needs. I'm incredibly fortunate to have a friend like him who truly loves me for me. And now he wants to be free to go globetrotting.

I ask, "How on Earth are you going to afford to go travelling? I know your mum and dad have always given you everything you've wanted, but do you really think they're going to let their seventeen-year-old son go travelling around the world by himself?"

Jack never worries about things like that. His three brothers and two sisters moved out years ago and now have their own children. He enjoys being the baby of the family. Jack has always used the perks that come with being the youngest to his full advantage. He does however take his role of being fun uncle, a title he gave himself, very seriously. The house is often a bit crazy; generally, the kids are there most days as they know Grandma and Grandad always spoiled them. Jack's parents, Jenny and Mark, love to entertain, and their parties are unforgettable. Since the age of eleven, I've always been invited to their New Year's Eve party which is incredible, and they always make sure I'm comfortable.

"Hang on, what do you mean *you*? Don't you mean we?" Jack gets so excited about creating memories and trying new experiences together, that he very often forgets that I have goals of my own. My dream has been to be an actress on the West End. I have fond memories of when mum took me for a birthday treat to see *Joseph and The Amazing Technicoloured Dreamcoat* at the London Palladium. I knew I wanted to be a West End actor and see my name in big bright lights from that moment onwards. Ten years later, I can still remember all thirty-three colours of Joseph's coat. That needs to be added to my CV.

After waiting for everyone to get off the bus and making sure the driver remembers to lower the bus even though he did this not twenty minutes prior, Jack always walks with me from the bus stop to my tutor room, which is why he's had so many detentions for being late that I've lost track.

As I walked into tutor, I noticed Josie and Emma were already there sitting on stools with a space between them. Our tutor room is a science lab which is actually quite annoying because we have stools instead of chairs. I'm always worried about falling off as my balance isn't always the best and I have tendency of laughing way too much with the girls.

As I steady myself on the stool next to the girls someone says, "Careful, I don't want to pick you up of the floor again."

One time in Year 8, Josie and I trying to entertain ourselves by seeing if we could throw pieces of paper into the bin that was opposite us. Somehow, I managed to overextend my arm which resulted in me losing my balance and falling off the stool. Luckily, Josie was there like she always is and helped me up without making it a big deal. It was mortifying having to have the girls pick up from the floor whilst everyone else was cracking up.

As usual, Josie is putting on her third layer of powder foundation. In her words, she would otherwise look like an alien. I would love to look like her with her naturally blonde wavy hair and the way she can somehow make her school uniform look like it should be at a Paris fashion show. Emma is the complete opposite; there's a tomboy look about her. She always looks like she could fall back to sleep by always having her head on the desk face down and making the occasional groan.

The support that I have from my friends is invaluable. They understand what I need help with but always do it as discreetly as they can. My confidence has definitely grown because I've got such amazing people around me. Although, there's always a constant argument about who will get my disabled badge in their car when we're finally allowed to drive. I first met Josie and Emma at primary school. Since then, we have been inseparable. I may not have the biggest friendship group in the world, but I'd rather have only a couple of true friends than fake friends who ditch me when my disabilities get in the way. I've always preferred someone asking me what disabilities I have rather than making assumptions, no matter how blunt it may be.

As I reluctantly drag myself to Key Skills, I have to remind myself it's better to get the worst lessons out of the way first. Our assignment for the lesson is to write about what we wish to achieve in the next five years. I frantically start writing on my piece of paper that I want to apply and audition for RADA (Royal Academy of Dramatic Arts) in London. This is one of the best performing arts schools in the country. Hopefully, then I'll be able to achieve my dreams of appearing on the West End. I find drama so therapeutic; it means that I can be someone else for a while, instead of the girl with a disability. It's so annoying that because of my cerebral palsy my hands aren't able to keep up with my brain. I have been offered a laptop numerous times before but every time I've declined as that would make me stand out even more.

I then explain how I want to make the sector more inclusive to the next generation. Mr Long walks around the classroom, observing our progress. I can feel his presence as I pour my career goals onto a single sheet of paper.

Mr Long smiles at me. "That's one thing I admire about you, Amy. You have always had such big goals. Even if they are one in a million!"

I place my pen down rather purposefully on the table, take a deep breath. "I'm sorry, sir, but what do you mean by that?"

He looks puzzled as to why I'd challenged him on this passing statement. Not breaking my stare, he seems flustered and starts to stutter his words.

"No, no, what I meant to say, that it's tough for anyone to get into the acting business. The chances of achieving stardom are small. I'm aware of the intense competition within the acting business that even the best of the best can struggle to get anywhere."

"I'm sorry, but how brain washed are you?" Hannah, my arch nemesis, never misses an opportunity to take a dig at me.

"Oh yeah, well at least I have dreams."

I try to compose myself to deal with challenging him. "Are you, by any chance, implying that because I've got a disability, I shouldn't shoot for the stars and achieve my dreams because surely that's not your role as a teacher? Isn't your role to help and support us students to reach our full potential? I can't change who I am. Although there are some days I want to, believe me. I'm extremely offended that you've assumed that I won't be able to do this. Now I would really appreciate it if you would keep your opinions to yourself, OK? I'm very conscious that the road ahead will be tough, and there are so many uncertainties. But you know what nothing worth having in life ever comes easy. Doctors told me I wouldn't be able to walk, and by the looks of it, I managed that! Let me ask you this: would you say that to someone who doesn't have a disability?"

He was bright red in the face; a single bead of sweat starts to trickle down his cheek.

I am utterly disgusted that those words had actually come out of his mouth. It's not just teachers that accidentally do this, but most professionals as well. One speech therapist I had when I was younger thought it was cute that I wanted to be an actress when I grew up. Unfortunately, over the years, it's just something that I have had to learn to accept.

"I'm so sorry, Amy. It wasn't my intention to cause offence. I guess there are some things that even I still need to be educated about. I guess we are always learning, and it's people like you that make the world a better place for correcting people when they make a misjudgement." He looks up at the rest of the class. "Right, can you all finish the sentence that you're on? We will pick this up again next week, thank you, year 13."

My mum has taught me always be proud of who you are and stand up to people who try and drag you down. We are all unique, and that should be celebrated instead of being discriminated against.

I despise Key Skills and feel that I don't need it; P.E. is even worse; it's definitely not my favourite day of the week. I find it so annoying that Mr Davies will always come over to me and have what he likes to call a quiet word every lesson.

"Hello Amy, thanks for joining us. We're going to practice serving today. Are you going to be alright with that? If not, I can always adapt it for you."

I'm well aware that I use a walking frame, but my balance and coordination isn't so bad that I'm unable to do any physical activity. Although, getting your own changing rooms certainly is a silver lining. As I reluctantly make my way to the tennis court, Josie and Emma are already there waiting for me.

Mr Davies stands in the middle of the tennis court. He's rocking his usual turquoise tracksuit paired with a white vest and a whistle around his neck. He looks like he's walked off the set of the movie *Fame.*

"Amy, what did I just say?" he asks.

I know I am in trouble. I have to think of a justifiable response and quickly. "Ummm, either hit the ball or catch the ball, sir?"

He doesn't look amused in the slightest. "Amy, you need to start listening if you want to pass my class, please."

My classmates are all in fits of laughter. This is why I need to learn to think before I speak or at least sometimes.

Mr Davies continues to show the serve that he wants us to try and then practice with a partner. Josie and Emma always wait for me after the lesson as they know I take longer than the other girls. I have been offered one-to-one support many times over the years, but honestly, there's not a lot they would need to do.

Jack is slumped against the door waiting for me outside the main hall. Jack always is so sly with helping me with getting lunch so that I don't have the embarrassment of asking a teacher for help.

"Have you thought about what you're doing for half term?" he asks whilst we were making our way over to the table. We've only just gone back to school after the summer break, and already, he's thinking about another week off.

"No, I don't know. Probably just stay at home and catch up on all the revision and homework we will probably have."

Jack is waiting for the laugh to follow this. I think Jack sometimes forgets that I've got to work twice as hard to keep up with everybody else.

Jack suddenly stops tucking into his cheese and pickle sandwich when he realises that I'm being serious. "Come on, Amy, live a little. The world is our oyster!"

Jack has always been one to do the fun stuff first and then worry about his grades. He's never been one to want to be the highest achiever. He always he does what he does just to get what he needs, and that's enough for him. It's not like Jack is going to be an open-heart surgeon.

"What do you have in mind? I'm not saying that I'm going to do them, but by that devilish look on your face, I can tell it's something epic," I ask.

He is rubbing his hands together and jiggling in his seat

due to sheer excitement. “Well, there’s a new rock-climbing place at the leisure park. Why don’t we try it out! However, if we do, we better book it quick.” I am very apprehensive about this, and he continues, “Look, I know this year is so important to you, and RADA is at the forefront of your mind, but trust me, everybody needs to have a little fun every once in a while. Also, Amy, I know you like the back of my hand and know that if you get too stressed, you’re going to make yourself ill.”

I can’t fully understand why he wants to do this. I’m so appreciative of him because he always pushes me to be the best version of myself. He makes sure that I’m healthy and happy, which is why I can’t imagine my life without him.

Unfortunately, I’ve lost friendships over the years. I think it’s because some people don’t see past the walking frame or can’t deal with me having a seizure. So, I think it’s easier for them to just cut me out of their life completely. Having a disability isn’t a choice but how others choose to accept you is.

Jack knows he can make fun of my disability all day long because when I need him, he’s always there. I sit back on my chair for a second and think about how I can word my answer without giving off too much sarcasm; however, that will never happen.

“Yeah, we could and also, while we’re doing that, we could also find a cure for my disability or see a rainbow-coloured unicorn!” I smile.

"Amy, you know you can do this, remember you're the girl who was told she couldn't walk!" He always uses this reason when he really wants me to do something. He knows I can't trump it.

By the time I get home from school, I am absolutely SHATTERED! No surprise that Mum is standing by the front window. I take a deep breath and open the door. "I'm home!"

I immediately threw off my coat and hung it up on the bannister, much to Mum's annoyance as she's always complaining about tidying up after me.

"How was your day? Nobody bullied you, did they?" She throws her arms around me so tightly, it is suffocating.

I am expecting this from Mum, but it feels weird because this is the last time it will be my first day of the new year. Realising this feels incredibly daunting.

My feet are absolutely killing me due to not having worn my splints for that long in six weeks. As I undo the two Velcro straps that keep them in place, it's such a relief and immediately recline on the sofa. I grab the TV remote and start flicking through the channels; *Friends* is on any time of the day. Mum stands over me, waiting for any kind of answer.

"Mum, calm down; everyone was nice like they are every year! It's not like my friendship group has changed in the last seven years, and I highly doubt it's going to change any time soon! Plus, we both know that even if anyone did bully me, Jack wouldn't put up with any of it."

After reassuring her that I don't need counselling on the first day of the year, I decide it would be best to get on with the mountain of coursework that I already have. It's never a good idea to get behind on the first day of the year but being on the phone with Jack makes it a little bit easier.

"How was your mum when you got home?" he asks even though he is already laughing because he knows the answer.

"Sixty questions in sixty seconds!"

Jack always finds it hilarious how in your face my mum can be sometimes, but it's always done with love.

chapter 2

Waking up the following day is somehow even harder. After checking my timetable yesterday, I notice that I've got a new teacher for English. Great! One of the most important lessons in my timetable; this isn't going to go well. Typically, they take one look at me and then talk to me like I'm an idiot or just ignore me. I would much prefer teachers ask me what I am capable of rather than make assumptions, which are usually incorrect.

Due to the size of my walking frame, I have to go the long way around the classroom. I sit down in my usual chair next to Connie. Much to my surprise, given it's still the first week of term, she has a very excited look on her face. Connie and I aren't exactly the best of friends, but she definitely makes our English lessons far more entertaining.

"Did you hear about Hannah?" she asks.

"No?"

I know that this will be gossip gold, by the sheer look of excitement on Connie's face.

Hannah and I have never seen eye to eye. She is far too entitled as she comes from a wealthy family and her father is a governor on the school board, so she thinks she can do anything she wants and still get away with it. When we have spoken, which isn't a regular occurrence, she always talks to me like an idiot. Which is why I do it back to her; it's obviously the only way she can manage human interaction.

"She waxed both her eyebrows off last night."

I instantly burst into fits of laughter. After all these years, finally, she can have a taste of her own medicine. Hannah has never accepted me because, in her words, I look different. Right on cue, she walks into the room; you can tell that she has tried to cover it up by using an eyebrow pen. Her technique isn't exactly pro-makeup artist level, so it looks like two slugs above her eyes.

She looks in my direction. "Oh yeah, well, I can still get any guy I want unlike some people who are still sadly single. Don't worry, Amy, I'm sure someone who obviously has a low standard will sweep you off your feet."

"Well, based on the guys that you go out with, like the one that needed to be told you have to peel an orange before you eat it. I'd much rather be single."

She stamps her feet under the table because she has got nothing else to throw back at me. Josie and I high five. I've won this one.

Eventually, Mr Roberts calls attention to the class by clearing his throat and then sets us an assignment to write a short explanation of a book we read over the summer break. He looks over in my direction and starts to walk over to my chair. "If there's anything you need support with, like understanding the question, just let me know."

I think about throwing a sarcastic comment back to him, but decide not to; usually, it doesn't end well for me. I just wish there was a way for teachers to understand the kind of discrimination I go through daily just because I've got a disability.

By the time I get home, Mum is standing by the door waiting for me. Although today, she doesn't have the warm, inviting look on her face. She stands with her phone in her hand and her look is similar to the one I got when she found out I snuck out of the house to go to a party.

"Your head of year has just been on the phone, young lady."

The only thing I know to do in this situation is to make a joke. "Oh, is this finally the call to say that I've been appointed head girl?" I laugh. Even I don't believe what I had just said. I should learn to keep my mouth shut every once in a while.

"No, he said that you have been back chatting Mr Stevens." She has the patience of a saint. "How many times do I have to tell you, back chatting a teacher or in fact anyone won't get you anywhere?"

Mum folds her arms and let out a sigh of despair.

"Mum, how would you feel knowing every day that you get sympathetic looks because you're different or because you don't have the look? I have a disability that I can't change no matter how much I want to. Most days, I'm so proud of who I am and where it has got me. Unfortunately, there are the odds day when I wish I didn't have this." I purposefully point to my walking frame. Despite what I've just said, my frame has always been my secret weapon because it constantly remains of how far I've come and how far I still want to go. "Mum, you have no idea how strong I have to be every day not to let my disabilities win, the things I would give not to be disabled!"

I look back at her as tears are streaming down her face. Her body shakes with emotion. I know this is painful for her to hear, but I need to make my point. "Or having the responsibility of making sure that I don't forget to take my tablets, or I realise this is a bit extreme but what if I have a seizure and don't wake up. Anyway, Mum, I didn't actually say anything. I just ignored him. I thought about it, though."

"Amy, when they gave you to me in the hospital with all the tubes and wires, I wondered and worried how your life would pan out. The doctors told me you wouldn't walk, talk, or even have a chance of having an independent life. Well, hunny, I think you've proved them wrong. You've always shown everyone and anyone that your disabilities or difficulties would never define you. Now I can't get into your head and understand what everyday life is like for you. Being your mum, I'm so proud that my only daughter has so much determination and drive to get the most out of her incredible life. Amy, sometimes you don't have to say anything. I've seen the looks you can give and trust me; they speak a thousand words."

I'm taken aback by what she's saying and know that she has seen my struggles first-hand. She has always told me that in order for change to happen, we need to be the ones that make that change for the better.

"I completely understand that you always want to make sure that your voice is heard, and you're never treated any differently to your friends. You are so educated about disabilities and ensuring that everyone gets equal opportunities, no matter who they are. All you've wanted your whole life is to be like everybody else. We are all different; I can assure you that everyone has things that they would want to change given the opportunity. I'm so proud that you've always got that fire in you and never take no for an answer. I absolutely love that my daughter wakes up every day and sticks two fingers up to the world." Her face lights up with pride.

"I am so privileged to call you, my daughter. You're certainly my favourite." She always knows how to make me smile. "Unfortunately, Amy, you need to learn sometimes to keep your head down and mouth shut. We both know you're so capable of achieving your dreams. I know why you did what you did because I would've done the exact same thing or perhaps even worse when I was your age. You've overcome so many obstacles and somehow have the determination to achieve more. However, this is one of the most important years, and if you want to get into drama school, this can't happen again. Like I've always said it's better to try and fail than to not try at all. We both know you're fully capable of reaching your full potential so please keep your head down and no more back chatting teachers. You hear me, young lady?"

I know she's right; she always is. Mum is always so wise with her words, raising me all by herself can't have been easy.

"So, what do I do just let people walk all over me?" I have fought my whole life to be treated like everybody else.

"No, definitely not, sweetie ,and I don't think you would ever let someone do that to you. Although sometimes you need to pick your battles. We both know you're such a fighter, but sometimes the strongest thing to do is just letting things wash over you because it's not worth it."

Her strength is inspiring, and she does it all with a smile on her face. From the age of two, it was just her and me. From what she's has told me about my dad, he was an alcoholic. I don't really remember spending any time with him and in my eyes I come from a single parent family. Mum very rarely mentions him but from what I've heard he was abusive both physically and emotionally to her. After years of going through this day in day out, she finally got the support she needed to kick him out for good.

She had to find the strength to take care of me by herself, which is why we now refer to him as my sperm donor. I'm confident that that's where I get my stubbornness from. I would sometimes ask where he was, and Mum wouldn't really say much, just that I couldn't visit him.

chapter 3

Even though a week has passed, Mum's words have definitely stuck with me. She's seen the struggles I've faced first-hand and still given me all the support I needed and more; she's a real-life superhero.

Mr Roberts starts the English lesson by explaining what our A-Level exam will consist of. He explains all the reading materials we will see before sitting the exam. Due to being in a higher tiered class, we have to sit an English language exam plus an English literature exam.

English is the only lesson that I actually feel comfortable with even the idea of an exam. Mum keeps telling me that instead of thinking of the mammoth task of an exam, take it lesson by lesson. I focus on writing my essay explaining how the story of Romeo and Juliet could exist within the 21st Century. Although this is a classic love story, I include the idea that this can happen even when everything is against them, including family values and religious beliefs. I base the concept on the unlikelihood of two individuals coming together from different classes within the U.K.. After looking through my textbook to appreciate the point that individuals who come from different classes can have different opinions about money, health and values which could then put pressure on the relationship.

I've always tried to make sure that I connect and have relationships with people from all different walks of life. From a young age, Mum would always teach me about how we are all different and these differences should be celebrated not discouraged.

Maths with Mrs Evans is my worst nightmare. She only pays attention to the students who excel in her lesson and ignores the rest of us. This doesn't help when you're just months away from sitting one of the most important exams of your life. The other annoying thing she does is that sometimes I will have a personal assistant in lessons, and she will talk to them instead of me. Does that mean that my personal assistant wants to take the exam for me? I find it incredibly irritating that just because I have physical disabilities, somehow, I am treated differently. Whatever happened to inclusion and diversity? I'm sure that teachers are meant to be there to cater to the needs of each and every student to make sure they reach their full potential, or at least that's what Mr Perkins tells me every time I make a complaint. I can't help being disabled; I've tried.

Having assembly after lunch is handy, works off the food coma. Today Mr Perkins appears to be very excited for some weird reason, oh the sad life of a teacher! We have to sit in tutor groups, and it's meant to be boy, girl, boy, girl. Josie, Emma, and I somehow always sit together. Mr Perkins always waits till everyone sits down till he enters; he must think he's so important.

"Good afternoon, everyone!"

It's expected that we respond with the same greeting. However, after doing this for the past seven years, there's little to no enthusiasm from anyone.

"As I'm sure you are all aware, we are yet to appoint our head boy and head girl, which is why I'm pleased to announce this year, we are opening up the opportunity for this position to anyone. I know in the past that this role has been awarded to those who are high achieving. As we strive to be inclusive within the whole school, so change is essential. All that is required from those who would like to apply is a written letter explaining why they would be a suitable candidate.

"The role of head boy and head girl is something that should not be taken lightly. It consists of great responsibility and constant representation for the school. Successful candidates should also be aware that they will be a role model for younger students at all times. We will also be looking for individuals who have tremendous leadership skills to guide fellow prefects and ensure that their duties are completed to the highest standard."

Something suddenly ignites inside of me. Straight away, it feels like I had a new lease of life. I know that this will look amazing on my RADA application and my CV. After all, I certainly consider myself a good role model; given that I haven't had the best hand in life, I've done alright.

"After interviews have taken place, a panel of teachers and the school's governing body will then come to decision of who we feel is the best-suited candidate." For the first time in an assembly, I am focused entirely on Mr Perkins. "So, I would like to wish each and every one of you the best of luck."

As I make my way to drama after assembly, I have this new lease of energy that I need to release. For this lesson, we are working on our devised pieces that would go towards our final grade. Miss Stevens is new to the school this year. She has just graduated from RADA. I need to suck out of her any information I possibly can to have the best chance of getting a place. Fortunately, I'm never shy of asking a question. I am unsure what question to start with though: How many times did you audition? What was your most memorable moment? Did you get lead roles in any productions?

I know I just have to pick one question to start. "Miss Stevens, I'm Amy, hi. I was just wondering what the audition process was like to get into RADA?"

She looks a little frazzled as the lesson has barely begun; already, she is in the hot seat. As she sits on the edge of her chair facing us. I can tell she was struggling to come up with an answer. "Good morning, Amy. It's a pleasure to have you in my class. Are you asking for a friend?"

Her smile is warm and infectious.

"No, I'm asking for me. I'm applying for RADA. I want to become a West-End actress."

"I'm sorry, but to get into drama school, especially one of the best in the country, you need to have the right physique." She turns to face the rest of the glass. "Now, could we all find a space in the studio, and we're going to start the lesson with some character development exercises."

I am in complete shock that these words have come out of her mouth. I've had some teachers say that I'm incredibly ambitious but not get my hopes up too high. I am baffled. A teacher's role is to inspire and guide students in the right direction in life.

However, this one, much to my disbelief, has just insulted me directly to my face. "Are you saying I'm too disabled to be an actor? I wonder if anyone has said this to Warren Davis after being in *Star Wars*, one of the best film franchises of all time. Or Michael Phelps, one of the greatest athlete swimmers of all time who just so happens to have ADHD. Michael J. Fox, who is extremely verbal with his Parkinson's as well and yet did that stop him?"

Miss Stevens stands frozen while I am verbally vomiting

all these fantastic and inspirational icons that I hope to follow in the footsteps of some day.

Before she has time to reply, I am out of the drama studio, along the corridor and heading straight to Mr Perkins's office. Rage fuels me; I am fully prepared to use my walking frame as a battering to anyone who dares to get in my way. Miss Stevens is running behind, trying to catch up with me. She is apologising profusely the whole way there as she knows what is coming next. I am walking so fast along the corridor that one foot could easily catch under the other, leaving me flat on my face.

I don't even knock. Instead, I just let the door swing open in full force. "Mr Perkins, can I ask you a question?"

Before he can answer, I proceed. "I'm a little confused." I pause for a second.

"I thought that as a school, we pride ourselves on being inclusive and making sure that every student is valued and heard?" I am still standing in the doorway and very aware that several other students and teachers have suddenly stopped in their tracks to watch.

Mr Perkins looks stunned about what I had just said; however, his tone somehow remains calm. "Amy, why don't you have a seat, and we can discuss this?"

I am not moving until I get an answer.

He says, "You're correct there. We are committed as a school to making sure that every student is able to flourish safe and secure environment. We also like to create an environment throughout the school that is diverse and inclusive so that every student can reach the full potential."

This isn't a justifiable response and fails to impress me. I know it is the one that every teacher has memorised. Obviously, it is in place of having an honest and open conversation with students about one of the more significant issues of our generation.

"If this is the case and it's a shared commitment by the whole of the school, why did this we hire a teacher who just verbally abused me in front of EVERYONE!" I ask.

Yet again, I have left both teachers speechless as I'm claiming something that I'm fully aware Miss Stevens could lose her job over.

"Amy, that is quite an accusation and one that I cannot take lightly," he says as I stand there breathing heavily; my whole body is shaking with rage, which is never fun when you have a physical disability.

"Amy, I'm so sorry. It was a mistake, and if I could take back my words, I definitely would." Her words fail to impress me.

"I'm well aware and don't want you to take this lightly. I've just been verbally abused by a teacher," I look in her direction, "who should know better."

Miss Stevens stands next to me in floods of tears, but I don't even have an ounce of remorse and continue. "Let me ask you a question if this had happened to a person of colour or ethnic background, how would you respond?"

Mr Perkins looks rather uncomfortable. Suddenly, his body language is tense as he clicks his pen uncontrollably. I am breathing very heavily at this point and can feel a bead of sweat trickling down my face.

"Just like this accusation, we would take that very seriously, and a full enquiry would take place. We want every student at this school to feel safe at all times, no matter what they look like or where they come from," he says.

I am getting redder with every word that has fallen out of Mr Perkins's mouth. Still full of rage, I only hear half of what he has said. "So, does that mean that an investigation is not going take place?"

I stand there, not breaking eye contact with Mr Perkins while he is fumbling around, trying to find an answer. Again, Mr Perkins looks very stunned at my quick response, "N-NO, that's not what I'm saying. Amy, you have my full assurance that this will be dealt with appropriately and correctly."

"Let me speak to the senior management team. I will need both of you to present a written statement of your view of the incident. I will need Miss Stevens and each student who was in the lesson today to give written statements about their versions of the incident. This all needs to be completed by the end of the day."

Before he can even finish explaining the process, I interrupt, "Easy! She verbally insulted me, done!"

Mr Perkins takes a deep breath. After being my head of

year for seven years, he certainly has learned how to have patience with me, especially when I go off on one of my rants. "Amy, you know that's not how it works. Come on; you're a smart girl."

I know he's right, but I am still utterly outraged. I write down what has happened before and the words that have somehow fallen out of her mouth. I take a sheet of paper from his desk and walk out of the office without looking that bully in the eye. Why does this keep happening? I'm finally making progress and achieving my goals and yet I'm still knocked down for things that I are out of my control.

As I make through the front door after school, I'm overwhelmed with a mixture of emotions. I don't want to tell Mum about what had happened at school because I know it will panic her and she will definitely storm into school tomorrow morning demanding an apology. I decide to use this energy in a positive way and write my head girl application letter. There's so much that I've achieved over the last seven years, but my main goal is to make sure anyone no matter who they are is able to achieve their dreams.

chapter 4

After what feels like the longest start to the year ever, half-term has finally arrived. To my relief this means lie ins and lazy days, just what is needed. Reaching for the cold steel of my frame doesn't feel as daunting this morning as finally I can relax. Although, I can't help but still discuss with Jack our plans for the week as he hasn't stopped talking about rock-climbing for weeks. After doing so much research, he has even found somewhere that's accessible for me. I'm extremely torn between creating these amazing memories with Jack and resting at home because I know that's what my body needs. Just as I'm settling in to a *Scrubs* marathon, Josie texts.

Hey babe, I'm throwing a Halloween party at mine next Saturday; you in? xx

I love being a social butterfly, meeting new people, and

having fun. I am, however, very aware of constantly being judged just because I use a waking frame. Some disabilities can be hidden. Unfortunately, mine can't. I always try to come across as confident in the hope that people can see past my disabilities. Unfortunately, this isn't always the case and countless times before I've been ignored or made fun off for simply being me.

When you have a disability, especially one that's visible, I find that either people don't understand why I am like I am, or they just don't care. I would much prefer it if people just asked questions instead of making judgements. Is it that hard? Also, there are many things that I've got to consider when going to someone else's house. Can I fit my walking frame through the front door of their house? Will there be an accessible toilet that I can use? Will my friends have a better time if I'm not there? That way they won't have to constantly worry about whether I'm ok.

Social anxiety is something that I've battled with for years due to my disabilities. Although not going would make me feel even worse. I would constantly be thinking about what I would be missing out on. I have always felt that I'm so different from everyone else. No matter how many times my friends tell me that I'm Amy and they wouldn't want to be to be any different, I can't help but wonder will they talk about me if I'm not there?

What if Mr Right is there? I always laugh when this pops into my head. I grew up in the noughties, meaning that every television programme and movie we watched taught us that the one will just appear from nowhere. You would then spend the rest of your life with this person or as they say in the movies happily ever after.

After considering all my options for a while, I reply,

"*Yes I'll be there. Can Jack come?*"

Instantly I get a thumbs up emoji back from her. I stand up from my bed and turn off my TV where I've been watching reruns of *Scrubs* for the hundredth time. As I hold onto my frame to steady myself since my legs hadn't quite woken up, I think about how I am going to word this so Mum won't totally freak out. I am filled with nerves walking from the bedroom to the kitchen. Before I can chicken out and retreat to my bedroom, I take a deep breath to compose myself.

"Mum, I've just got a text from Josie." I hold onto my frame so tightly that my hands are going whiter and whiter by the second.

Before I can continue, she asks, "Oh, how is she? Josie, Jack, and Emma should come around for dinner this I could cook, or we could get a takeaway? How about pizza? Your favourite."

Mum's interruptions don't help me gear myself up for asking her.

"Mum, Josie's invited me to a Halloween party she's throwing this weekend, and I was wondering whether I can go, please?"

I don't want to tell her too much info because if she knows that it will be a bunch of teenagers drinking and dancing, it will be an automatic no. Mum stands there contemplating whilst continuing to load the dishwasher.

"Where is this party? Also, Amy how are you getting there and getting home?" She looks concerned which is understandable. It's her job to make sure that I'm safe. Oh, the joys of being a parent.

I take a big gulp. "The other side of town on Haven Way, and I was wondering whether you could drive me there? I'm sure I could get a lift home with Emma." Even though Mum has dropped me off at Emma's house many times before, I'm sure she loses track of who's who.

Haven Way is one of the poshest parts of town. Detached houses with beautiful lawns and a Range Rover or Bentley parked on the driveway. I'm sure a lot of houses also have swimming pools in their back gardens. Everything looks so perfect that it's almost as if someone goes around with nail scissors to every single strand of grass.

Mum is still standing the same spot, giving little to no expression so that I can't tell whether it would be a yes or no. "You can go on two conditions."

Only two? I was expecting a whole list. "Anything."

She proceeds, "You need to let me know when you're leaving and exactly who you are with. Also, I don't want you doing too much for the rest of the week. Do you hear me, Amy? Of course, I'll drop you off. What time do you need be there for?"

I am gobsmacked. "Um, I think seven, but I'll check and let you know. Thanks, Mum, love you." I kiss her cheek.

I was fully expecting Mum to demand a time that I needed to be home by. Before she can change her mind, I swiftly walk out of the kitchen and sit on the sofa to reply. That's one of the most annoying things about using a walking frame. I'm unable to walk and text. Now I know that's a minor detail, and I should be thankful that I can actually walk and move independently. However, a girl can still dream, right? Whilst lying on the sofa, I send a simple reply.

"I'm in! xx"

I know this will instantly spark excitement within Josie.

The hardest of all of this is going to be telling Jack. This isn't going to go down well, and I am almost more nervous telling him than I was telling Mum. My breath becomes deeper and deeper the more rings that go by. Unfortunately, it goes to voicemail; it briefly crosses my mind to tell him over voicemail. However, who lets their best friend down over voicemail? An hour has passed when I hear the car horn ringtone, it reads,

"Hey sorry I only just saw your missed call. I was playing football with Harry. What's up?"

I immediately ring him before I hesitate too much. I know this is going to hurt him considering how much he does for me.

"Hey, what's up? Sorry, I missed your call. Harry insisted

that we have a game before it's too dark. He keeps bugging me because he's got a really important game on Sunday, so he's been practising around the clock; the things I do for my nephews."

I wish he hadn't told me this as it's so much harder to let him down when he's being so sweet. "That's fine, umm you know we were going to do all those adventurous things this week?"

"Yeah?" He sounds concerned, which makes it even harder.

"Well, the thing is Josie and Emma have invited to this amazing party on Saturday night, and Mum has said that if I want to go, then I shouldn't be doing too much for the rest of the week."

Before I can tell him that I need to cancel our plans, he shouts, "BASICALLY, WHAT YOU'RE SAYING IS THAT YOU'RE BAILING ON ME, YOUR BEST FRIEND, TO GO TO SOME STUPID PARTY, THANKS, AMY!"

I burst into tears as he explodes down the phone. "I'm sorry, but this party is something that's happening on one night and the things that we had planned we can do at time!"

Even through this is the best excuse I have; I know it is nowhere near good enough. I also realise that crying whilst trying to make a point doesn't exactly make the situation any easier.

"I can't believe you, Amy! Why couldn't you just said, 'Thanks, but I already have plans,' or 'I'll have to check with the person with to see if they don't mind changing.'"

I know he is right, but every inch of my body doesn't want to admit it. The thing about Jack and I's friendship is that we are both as stubborn as each other. So that means that it's impossible for either to back down and admit we are wrong. When we do argue, it can go on for days until one of us eventually apologises.

"Jack, don't be like that! Look. I'm really sorry, but everybody else is going. If I could do it all, you know I would, but come on, neither of us want me to have a seizure." I don't normally play the disability card, but I am running out of options. "It's not like we need to go rock climbing on a particular day. I'm sure they could rearrange our slot."

"No, you're wrong about that, I told you I needed to book a slot as they were already filling up or has that now conveniently slip you mind? Hey, don't worry about me. It's fine, go and have fun! Don't try the epilepsy card with me, you know it never works."

I know by his tone of voice that it is nowhere near fine, but before I could make a comeback, he hangs up. I don't think I've ever been so angry with him. Why couldn't he just understand that this is important to me and the things that were already planned we could do another time? Even if he had booked a slot, I'm sure could be changed. It's not like the place was only open for one day!

I wasn't expecting him to take it this badly. I mean I knew he would be annoyed, but I thought he would understand, even if it was only a little bit. All I want to do is fix what I've messed up. Although deep down I still want to go to the party so, going back on my word isn't an option.

"Amy, darling, can I come in?" I know all she wants to do was help. I make a slight groan which Mum takes as an invitation to enter. She walks over to me and sits down beside me on the bed. "You okay, sweetheart?"

"Mum, why can't Jack just understand that sometimes we get invited to things that we simply can't turn down." My face smothers into my pillow. I know what I've just said sounds incredibly selfish.

Somehow, she manages to keep her cool and puts her arm around me. "Amy, I understand why you've done what you've done because when I was your age, I would have done the exact same thing. However, just take a step back and put yourself in Jack's shoes."

She pauses for a moment.

"Imagine if you organised something for the both of you, had it plan out for weeks and then at the last minute, he lets you down. Jack did tell you a couple of weeks ago that he needed to book the tickets because I remember you coming home and telling me. You've got to remember that Jack put a lot of thought into organising this for the both of you. I understand where you're both coming from, but unfortunately I think in this situation sweetie you're in the wrong." Mum looks reassuring as she places her hand on my knee.

"Then, Mum, why didn't you say that I couldn't go to

the party! Mum! Whatever decision I make, I'm going to let someone down. If I don't go to the party, then Josie and Emma are going to be disappointed, but if I go then I have to let Jack. I can't win!"

Mum looks disappointed and shocked.

"Oh no, Amy! You're not throwing this back in my face! The reason why I said this is because I hoped that you'd make the right choice, which clearly you DIDN'T! Amy, you don't how lucky you are that I'm this calm when you blow up. If I'd done what you've done to your grandparents, I would have been grounded and wouldn't be going to the party at all. Amy, you of all people know that sometimes life isn't fair but how you deal with it is the most important thing."

Mum is now standing over me, far from the reassuring, comforting look that she had not twenty seconds prior.

"Young lady, you're seventeen now, which means that not only do you need to make your decisions but also suffer the consequences when you make the wrong decision. Also, have a little respect for me please you have no idea how hard it is raising a teenager by yourself."

Whilst sulking like a three-year-old, I say, "So, basically, you're saying that this was a life lesson, Mum. Why couldn't we have done this at another time?"

Mum just smiles at me. "No Amy, because this way you will remember how your actions have impacted others, and hopefully this will teach you a lesson to not make these mistakes in the future."

She promptly walks out of the room so that it hits me harder. She also knows that I like to have the last word. I throw myself back on my bed. All I want to do is call Jack to apologise, but that would then mean that I would be going back on my word, I can't do that. Also, I know this rash decision would only make the situation worse.

Usually, the worst sound of the week is my alarm going off on a Monday morning. However, much to my relief it is half term so no deadlines and no rushing around for a whole week. I would love to spend all day in bed but I'm pretty sure that my epilepsy would not appreciate this. I get my tablet box from the shelf and start popping out the threes that I take every morning. I'm so used to taking medication by now that I can almost do it without water, but I know that isn't best thing to do. I grab a glass of apple juice and start taking them. Whilst doing so, I expect to get a text from Jack just like every morning. Unfortunately, it doesn't come. This can only mean he's still mad at me. However, knowing Jack, if I ring him and explain everything, then surely this would all blow over. We would then be okay because surely that's what best friends do forgive and forget, right?

As I started go call him, I have a funny feeling that it will go to voicemail.

"Hi, this is Jack. Sorry I can't get to the phone right now please leave me a message and I will get back to you."

I contemplate for a second whether or not to leave a message, but suddenly this decision is made for me.

"Hey! It's me; look, I know I've really upset you and I completely understand why you were so annoyed when I told you, but this is silly! Call me back if you want." That is all I can do. I've now just got to hope that he gives me a chance to explain myself. As I carry on with my day and try and keep myself busy, I know that if I just keep staring at my phone, I will go crazier than I already am.

Finally, I hear car horn from my phone and breathe a sigh of relief. At least he's reached out to me. I slump back onto my bed and slide the phone unlocked.

"Hello, are you free this afternoon? Can we meet at the park, say just after 1?xx"

Well, that wasn't the response I was expecting at all. I thought it would say that everything was fine, but at least this is a start. I message Mum as she is now at the local café where she works lunchtimes but know she will be home while I'm out. She's done the jobs for years. She started working there back when I was still in primary school so that she would have something to do in the day but still be able to pick me up.

Her manager has always been so understanding of my disabilities. She doesn't even bat an eyelid when Mum must drop everything because I've had a seizure, which she has had to do several times over the years.

I only have an hour to work out how I am going to fix this and get Jack to forgive me. Unfortunately, the person who usually typically helps me with these situations is the one that's mad at me.

Before I know it, I need to leave the house and walk the short distance to the park, which is right by the bus stop. Fortunately, the neighbours are out, the last thing I need is their judgemental looks. Living in a village, you soon learn that everybody knows everybody else's business and keeping things private is almost impossible.

As I walk onto the football pitch, which is next to the park, Jack is already there. He's waiting for me on one of the picnic benches next to the swings. This sight brings back so many incredible memories of summers when we were kids and not having a care in the world. I remember one summer where I'd gained a bit more balance and thought I could go on the swings independently without someone putting their hand on my back to keep me stable. Unfortunately, this didn't go to plan and after lifting my legs of the ground for a brief second, I immediately fell back onto my bum with my legs dangling in the air.

He has a shy and quiet look on his face, which was very out of character for him. The autumn breeze brings a chill to the air. The park is so quiet that it's unnerving. Usually, there are kids on the swings or a football match going on, but today, nothing. I walk over to him and sit down without saying a word. I feel so awkward and am constantly scratching my arm which is the one thing I do when I'm nervous or uncomfortable. Unfortunately, Jack knows this trait of mine.

"Hey." Jack continues to stare down at the ground with his grey hoodie covering part of his face. I'm so glad that he started the conversation because it felt like an eternity that we were sitting there in silence.

We both took a deep breath and apologised at the exact same time. Immediately breaking into fits of laughter.

Being the gentlemen that he is, Jack lets me go first.

"I should've never thought about letting you down because, it's you." I think Jack is a bit surprised with what I've just said because he doesn't say anything. Instead, he just gives me the biggest hug ever.

"So, we're all good?"

As he let me go, he tells me no and pauses for a second as he knows his answer sends me into panic mode. "We're better than good."

He pulls me in once more, and as always, I feel safe and protected when I was with him.

"You may drive me crazy and it's definitely easier arguing with a brick wall," he says. He always knows how to make me smile. "I hate to admit it, I wouldn't have you any other way. Well, maybe a bit better at football."

Jack always makes me crack up the most at things that shouldn't be funny.

We head back to my house and the front door is unlocked, hopefully meaning that Mum is home. I shout "I'm home" whilst putting my keys away. Jack decides to join in as well.

Mum suddenly flies around the corner and gives Jack the biggest hug as if she hasn't seen him in years. Mum doesn't ask whether or not Jack is staying for dinner. She instead tells him he is, as she was making his favourite, lasagne. I don't have a say in the matter, which I don't mind at all.

The rest of the week goes by without a hitch. Jack only goes home to get more clothes or if the kids ring six times in a row, insisting that he come home for a game of football or rugby. Somehow, I end up being roped into these games as well. Playing sports isn't a strong point with me. However, Jack always makes it fun. He's the only person in my life that can do the patronising clap, without me getting offended, even when somehow, I manage to score a goal.

chapter 5

I have my outfit all planned out for tonight, a simple but elegant black skirt with a white lacey top paired with chunky black boots. I'm unable to wear lacey sandals as my splints won't fit inside them. Which is why I get to wear trainers to school, always a silver lining to everything.

Josie let me know yesterday that if Jack was able to tag along, he was more than welcome to. Jack took this invitation more than willingly as it meant an evening without his nieces and nephews. Mum had offered to take me to the party, but Jack insisted that his mum, Jenny, would pick me up on the way through. I think he was still making up for the other day even though it was partly my fault. Jack's dad Mark wasn't impressed as all the kids wanted a sleepover at Grandma's and Grandad's house that night as well.

When the car pulls up on the drive, Jack gets out of the

car wearing a blue shirt and black jeans. He walks around to the other side of the car and opens the door.

"Wow! You can actually make an effort when you want to!" I say.

After waiting for me to safely get into the car, he picks up my frame and folds it into the boot. Josie's house is about a twenty-minute drive away, which means that I have plenty of time to wind Jack up about whether or not he will get "lucky." Jack has never really been a lady's man and hasn't been in any serious relationships. He's had a couple of flings in the past, but nothing's really come of it. Although, he has always made it clear that if the opportunity should arise, then he wouldn't pass it up; what a gentleman!

As we walk through the front door, I am hit by a wall of people. Even though Josie is one of my best friends, I hardly know anyone here. The deafening noise of drum and bass music, Josie's favourite, is overpowering. I'm so glad Jack went in front of me to get through the living room as it seems that everyone else was well over six feet, so I definitely would've got squashed. People stop their conversations and just stare as I walk by. This is why I thought about not even coming. Eventually, we make it through to the living room, where Josie is standing with a bunch of girls who I don't recognise.

"Hey! It's my favourite girl! Come in! Everyone this is Amy! There is plenty of talent in here! If you know what I mean!" Josie isn't aware of the volume of her comment that was meant to be discreet. Everyone, not just at the party but probably in the whole neighbourhood, knows what she meant! Even though Josie is drunk and half the things she said don't even an ounce of sense, she's not wrong about the talent in the room. Although, I have no plans to make a fool of myself tonight and actually say this to anyone.

Josie and I are polar opposites in terms of talking to men. Single or taken, if Josie finds them attractive, she will make it known to them and everyone else. Which is why many girls don't really like her as she has caused relationships to break up. Her response to this is obviously the relationship wasn't strong enough in the first place. Depending on how much alcohol she's had depends on what version of Josie you get. Somehow, she always manages to pull at every party we go to and then we never see the guy again.

I'm much more reserved and quiet. I find the idea of talking to a guy I find attractive absolutely terrifying. I never know what to say. In the few instances that I have spoken to a guy, I'm constantly thinking about whether or not they're just doing it for a joke.

"I'm so glad your mum let you come. It wouldn't have been the same without you," Emma says, hugging me tightly like she's relieved that I actually showed up. I'm so glad that at least one of my friends knows how to handle their drinks.

"Yeah, me too, oh, thanks for reminding me." I reach for my bag on my frame. "I need to let I'm here. Otherwise, she'll kill me!"

"I adore your mum. You know she only does it because she cares. Plus, I don't think it would just be you getting killed. She would drag us all in for questioning."

I get so self-conscious about drinking just Coke. Jack has always said that I should just pretend that it's got vodka in it and frequently points out all the stupid things I do without being off my face. Jack certainly makes up for me not drinking. We aren't even here an hour yet and already he's three ciders in.

Josie changes the playlist to noughties pop; the first track "Reach" by S-Club, a classic. As soon as the first beat drops, the whole house erupts. Josie and Emma surround me so that I don't get knocked over. A little later in the evening, Jack, Emma, Josie, and I are sitting on Josie's large L-shaped sofa, trying to put the world right. Emma and Josie just fall about laughing. They are too drunk to understand the point of the conversation.

Suddenly, I turn my head and there he is. I have no idea where he's come from. I'm assuming heaven. He's gorgeous and way out of my league! I slowly look back at Josie and Emma, whilst displaying the biggest smile. I don't have the best poker face.

"Who's that?" I ask Emma, using my head to gesture where I am referring to without making it look too obvious.

She looks up at him, smiles and then looks back at me. "Oh, that's Jason he's one of our friends. We met him at a football match last year. Why?!?"

I continue to smile and give him quick glances before looking back at Emma as I don't want to look like a complete freak.

Emma starts to get extremely excited. "And yes, he's single before you ask!"

This forces me smile to grow even wider.

Before I pluck up the courage to go over to him as I am terrified of being judged, I observe him for a few moments. His jet-black hair is messy. It looks as though every single strand of hair has been placed in a specific place to give that perfect but rough look. I find myself getting lost in his blue eyes. He's rocking a black shirt and chinos. Always a tick for me when a guy dresses well. I am imagining myself cuddling into him. He stands up against a wall displaying his infectious smile, all whilst holding a beer that looks perfectly placed into his hand. I'm still getting lost in his incredible bright blue eyes. I can hear a noise in the distance. It is almost like I'm underwater in my own perfect little world, where nothing else matters but this astoundingly gorgeous guy and me.

"Amy, Amy! Earth to AMY!"

"Either you go and talk to him as you obviously want to, or I'll do it for you." She is right, also I know Emma doing it for me wouldn't going to go down well.

But I say, "I don't know what you're talking about."

"Yes, you do." She gives me a gentle nudge.

Emma is already on her third cider which is the worst

thing for her drink. I have better chances of him actually talking to me if Emma's cat did it. As I am trying to work how I am going to start a conversation with him, I'm suddenly standing next to him. It's too late. There is no backing out now.

My palms begin to feel sweaty as they are slipping off the grips of my frame. My brain is telling me, "Okay, now you have to say words," a moment passes, "any words will do! Come on, you know so many of them!" My face is becoming redder and redder by the second. I keep telling myself, "You can do this. I hoped I was doing in my head instead of out loud."

Eventually, a squeaky hi leaves my mouth and it's way too high and definitely not a smart first move. Now there is no backing out even though all I want to do is run away and hide. After a few seconds of sheer panic and embarrassment, luckily, a smile appears from him.

"Hi Amy, right? I'm Jason."

He already knows my name, result!

"Yeah, hi, wait, how do you know my name?"

He continues to smile.

"Sometimes when someone is so amazingly perfect and absolutely stunning, you just know even before they have introduced themselves, or I overheard your friend over there." He gestures his cup over to Emma and smiles at her whilst I let out a little giggle. "However, I thought the first one sounded a lot cooler. Plus, your smile is so infectious it was hard not to notice you."

I don't say anything; I just smile at him like a crazy person. He must think I'm a freak. I have various questions circling my brain. It feels like I am playing that hook a duck game at the fair. I just have to pick one at random and hope for the best.

"So, Emma said you and her brother play football together? How long have you played for?" Even though I didn't really want to have a conversation about football as I know nothing about it, it's worth the effort because he is so hot.

"I've played since I was a kid; yeah, I nearly made it to a professional level. Unfortunately, my parents wanted me to have a proper career, so I now only play once a week".

I again feel like a complete idiot for asking these questions, I think he could tell I don't do this often. Seriously I think I need to start listening to the girls more because they make it out that talking to guys is easy. Unfortunately, based on this situation, it is far from this. Although it's working as A, he hasn't left yet, and B, he was still laughing, but in a good way, well, I hope.

"Can I get you another drink?"

"Oh, that would be lovely. I'll have a—"

"Coke? Diet or full fat? I take note of the little things when someone is this attractive. I'll be right back. Don't go anywhere."

"Full fat please."

As he walks away, he turns back and winks, all whilst displaying his astounding smile.

I know I need to calm down before he comes back and sees how much of an idiot I actually am. I thought he would judge me on not drinking, but it didn't seem to faze him at all. For the first time, I feel relaxed around a guy that isn't Jack. I usually get super nervous around guys as it's not like I can hide my disabilities. I always worry about how they react when they see the frame or how I walk.

Emma and Josie ae still standing a short distance from me. As I look in their direction, they both give me the good old thumbs up and wink. So obviously, I am doing something right. He returns with our drinks and gives it to me in my left hand, my good hand. So, either he's very observant, or Emma has filled him in; either way, it means a lot. We continue chatting for quite some time until I notice that several people around us have left or moved to other places within the house.

"Shall we move this over to the sofa? My legs are getting a bit soar!" I'm glad he said it because I feel like such a wimp when making that excuse. He wraps one of his arms around me, which makes me feel safe, plus he smells amazing. We continue to chat about life, where we have grown up and where we would love to travel to someday. It is getting quite late, but I am not going to bail out and go home now.

He asks, "So, what are your plans for when you leave school then?"

Rarely, someone who I've just met is interested in my life. Typically, they just see the walking frame and I assume they think I don't have goals in life because I've got disabilities.

"I'm hoping to go to RADA next year, one of the best drama schools in the country. After completing my degree, I hope to become an actress on the West End". I usually get mixed responses when I tell people what I want to do after finishing school. Everyone knows how hard it can be to get into the performing arts industry, especially for someone with a disability.

"I hope you don't mind me asking, you don't have to say if you don't want to but, what are your disabilities?" He seems nervous and almost uncomfortable, but by this time, I'm used to it.

"Don't worry about it, Jason. I'm used to it by now. So, I have cerebral palsy, which is why I use a walking frame. I also have epilepsy, which is controlled by medication and also why I can't drink alcohol. It sucks that I can't blame the alcohol when I say stupid stuff!"

"I think you're amazing, how you've overcome obstacles within your life and have achieved so much. You're such an inspiration to others who think they can't do it and definitely a role model. It's incredible how you've shown that anything is possible when you put in the work. You're obviously a powerful, independent woman. It's a privilege to have heard your story, plus you're absolutely gorgeous."

He moves in closer to me and whispers in my ear, "You're

so sexy. It's hard not to let the mind wander. So beautiful and inspirational, you need a man who knows how lucky he is to be with someone like you. Fortunately, I know someone who could fulfil that role."

He stops talking for a brief moment, rests his forehead on mine and displays his irresistible smile. I know what is coming next and I am not complaining. He presses his soft, juicy lips against mine. He is a gentleman by showing that he's interested but not a complete monster. I don't want the moment to end. It is perfect. I suddenly notice Jack standing there very much in shock as to what he has just witnessed. Even though I know Jack doesn't even have the slightest crush on me, he is still very protective.

Jason stands, addressing Jack. "Hello mate, I don't believe we've had the chance of meeting. I'm Jason." He sits back down next to me and cuddles in closely.

I'm not sure how Jack will react because he's never really seen me with any other guy. However, being my best friend, he will be happy for me, right?

"Hi, I'm Jack, Amy's best friend. I see you two have already got acquainted." He sits down on the other side of me to Jason and puts his arm around me which is just a little bit awkward.

I feel like I am about to be squashed as neither of them was letting me go. The awkward silence doesn't exactly help. You could almost hear the crickets. I'm not sure why it is so awkward. In theory, Jack should be happy for me. I pulled first! This thought stays inside my head as it would only make the situation worse. I look over at Josie and Emma, unsure what to do. They don't seem to have any ideas either; what great support they are!

Jason is such a gentleman and tries to make small talk with Jack. "So, how long have you two known each other?"

Jack continues to stare Jason down.

"We've known each other since we were eleven. Haven't we, Jack?" I'm trying my best to get a conversation going whilst nudging Jack on the arm in the hope of getting him to say something.

I think it was sweet of Jason to at least try.

Jack asks, "So, who do you support?"

For once, I am actually glad that someone was trying to get Jack talking about football.

"Arsenal," Jason says. This isn't going to be good. "What about you?"

"Spurs. I guess somebody has to support that team. When was the last time you actually won something?"

Ignoring Jack's response, he says, "I'm actually quite thirsty. I'm going to get another drink. Amy, can I get you anything?"

Before I have a chance to respond, Jack says, "I bet you are! Given all the work you been doing."

I can't believe what my best friend had just said. I mean, I knew he wouldn't be jumping up and down for joy, but surely, he can understand. What right does he have to say whose throat I should or shouldn't have my tongue down!

"JACK! What do you think you're doing? Outside now!"

I can tell things are getting way out of hand, given the amount of alcohol that they have both have consumed.

"What do you think you're doing? That was totally uncalled for. How many beers have you even had tonight?" I ask. By the smell of his breath, I can tell that it was way too many. He is stumbling around, struggling to be coherent with his sentences. I can see in his eyes that he is obviously trying to work it out but doesn't have the mental capacity to do so.

"I'm sorry, Amy." Still stumbling around, he puts his hands around my waist to try and stabilise himself although, I'm not the best person to do that with. "He doesn't deserve you. He's a total idiot and a huge player who only wants one thing from you." Due to his current state, he just smiled sat this. "He will probably then toss you to the curb. Trust me, Amy, those guys shouldn't even be in your world. You can do so much better!"

His speech is slurred, and he is flapping his arms all over the place. Jack isn't the easiest to talk to when he's drunk as he frequently loses his train of thought. Usually, we end up having the same conversation at least three times before he gets all his points across. Jack only been drunk twice before, and it wasn't a fun experience for either of us. I still haven't told him all the things that he's done drunk, and I doubt I ever will.

I am confused because that is not the impression that I got of Jason. He seemed sweet. Jack pauses for a moment and seems to have sobered up suddenly. It is like he knows something that I don't and is trying to work out the best way to tell me. "Look, Amy, I didn't want to be the one to tell you this, but you're my best friend, the last thing I want to see is for you to get hurt."

Jack's energy completely changes, and I can immediately tell something was wrong.

Jack takes a deep breath. "Earlier, when I was getting you a drink, I overheard Jason and his friends talking about this new game that has been going around. Basically, the winner is the person who can pull the girl who has the most baggage, so he's basically just using you to win the game. I'm sure he'll then just walk away, leaving you broken! He's a total player and certainly doesn't deserve you. I'm extremely worried about you. Even though you're so strong-minded, you are vulnerable. I know that certain people like him will take advantage of this."

I am confused. This is not the impression I got of Jason at all. It's like we're talking about two different people. He seemed really sweet and generally interested in getting to know me. "Hang on! So, what you're saying is he did all that for a game. I don't understand. Then why did he want to know about my disabilities and RADA?"

"Well, Amy, unfortunately, there are people in this world that take advantage of good people. He's obviously not stupid because he's manipulated you to think that he actually likes you when really he's a fake, just using you to win a game."

I lose control of my emotions and actions; I immediately turned my frame around back into the house and stomped my way through to the kitchen. As I storm through the house, several people jump out of the way. Otherwise, I would've taken them with me. I am not even aware that Jack is right behind me until he almost goes over the back of my frame. Tears start to stream down my face. I am holding onto my frame so tightly my nails dig into my skin.

Jason and his mates have suddenly opened up the circle and are now staring at me. They are the classic group of lads at a party. The overpowering scent of Lynx Africa makes me gag; they are all wearing shirts in matching colours as if they're members of some boy band. I know Jason can feel my presence. He is about to put his arm around me but quickly retracts it. Everyone can tell that I am in no mood to be flirted with.

"So, did you win?!?" I ask.

Jason looks puzzled. "Um, babe, I'm not sure what you're talking about?" As all his mates are wolf-whistling, what gentlemen! "Hey, beautiful girl, why don't we go back to the sofa?"

He then starts to put his hands on my hips whilst biting his lip. Jack steps in front of me and puffs out his chest.

"You've got five seconds to get your hands off my best

friend. I know exactly what kind of game you are playing, and it isn't going to work. You have no idea how special Amy is to me. There's absolutely no way I'm going to let someone take advantage of her. Amy deserves to be treated with respect. You have no idea how hard she works to be the person she is. Obviously, you have no idea how to treat women. I would go to the ends of the earth to protect Amy, so I'm telling you now LEAVE HER ALONE!"

"Oh yeah, why the hell should I listen to you? Your best friend is so into me! I mean, why wouldn't she be!" He says this whilst looking me up and down. I feel sick.

Once more, I have to step in because Jack's mouth is always bigger than his bite, unfortunately.

Jack puffs his chest out again. "You should listen to me, mate. I'm doing you a favour and asking you nicely to piss off before I punch the living daylights out of you. Her standard is way above you; she's funny, kind, and brilliant." He says this whilst winking at me, which winds Jason up even more.

"I just have one question; did you mean anything you said to me before and was it all just to win this stupid game?" I need closure because I don't want to be anywhere near him again.

"Of course, I do, you're beautiful. I'm so attracted to you and think you're amazing."

I am not buying it.

"There is no way I'm letting a pathetic little boy like you

anywhere near her. I'm well aware that Amy can make her own decisions, and I know, of all people, how stubborn she can be. I've had the unfortunate pleasure of dealing with boys like you in the past. You may think she's beautiful and amazing, which she is, but you don't deserve her. You've got no idea what Amy has been through to get to where she is. Amy deserves a man, and you're nothing but a pathetic little boy, who won't take no for an answer." Jason's face suddenly turns a tomato colour and his fists clench, but Jack doesn't stop talking. "You may have been able to use these stupid little moves to lure girls in, in the past. This time, it's not going to work. I'm going to ask you one more time, leave her alone!"

I am standing between two men who were both over six feet and feel like they are about to cave in on me. I manage to get out just in time because a split second later, both the guys are on the floor wrestling each other. Everyone that is still here is heavily drunk. Which is why many deafening shouts and cheers are egging them on. I stand back to watch the guy who I thought cared about me fighting with the guy who's always there for me.

After several minutes there is suddenly a knock at the door; blue lights are flashing through the curtains. Josie goes to open it even though she knows what was going to be on the other side of the door. The rest of the house suddenly falls silent. You can hear a pin drop. Both Jack and Jason stand up quickly and straighten out their shirts. Jack's nose is bloody, and Jason has a black eye. The two police officers step inside and promptly make their way into the centre of the sitting room.

"We have had several calls this evening from surrounding neighbours saying there have a been a lot of loud noises coming from this residence. I would like kindly to remind you of what time it is. Therefore, could we please be considerate to the nearby residence."

Jack doesn't even look in my direction. He picks up his coat and heads to the front door. Jason is still standing in the middle of the room; he looks over at me and then leaves as well.

Fortunately, no charges are given. It is more of a polite reminder; at this point, we all think it would be best if we all went home before anything else happens.

I can't have been more shocked to what I have just witnessed. My legs are like jelly. This isn't how I imagined the night would end. Josie's mum offers to drop me back home on the way past. I know that calling Mum probably wouldn't be the best idea. Somehow, I remember to let her know.

"Just left the party, Josie's mum is dropping me off xx"

chapter 6

Due to all the dramas that unfolded last night, I'm exhausted. Scrolling through social media, I'm terrified that mum would find something and never let me out of the house again. Right on cue, I can hear her come bouncing through the door. I have my head buried under the duvet, although I know she's still there.

"Good morning!" Mum has always been a loud person. She knows I'm tired, which is why she's at a decibel higher this morning!

Even though I know I didn't have any alcohol last night, my head still pounds. I can only imagine this is what it's like to have a hangover. The bright autumn sun shines through the curtain.

Just as I am drifting back off to sleep, Mum sings out, "Good morning darling! It's a beautiful day. You got in late last night. It must've been a good party."

Instantly my eyes open wide, and I throw the duvet away from me. What does she know? Has she found out about Jason? I'm busted!

"So, how was last night, my lovely? I've made you some toast and a cup of tea. Do you want me to go and get your tablets from the kitchen as well?" She sits down on the end of my bed as I have yet to sit up.

I know she isn't going to leave until she gets an answer. "It was fun." My voice is croaky, and it hurts to talk. "Met some nice people, and Jack definitely looked after me," I say whilst replaying in my head everything that happened.

I'm hesitant to say anything else to Mum. These are the kinds of situations that Josie refers to as what she doesn't know won't kill her situations. Mum definitely doesn't need to know all the details. Much to my relief, there isn't a lot she can find on social media. If Mum knew that I kissed a guy last night that I barely knew and then turned out to be an actual creep who only wanted me to win a game, she would flip out.

Satisfied with my response, she leaves me to take my medication and eat my breakfast in peace. When I was younger, Mum would always insist that I open my mouth after taking them to prove that they had gone down. Josie calls.

"Hello, babe, what's up?" My voice is still a bit croaky after all the shouting and singing last night.

"I was just checking that you're ok. I'm really sorry for

even introducing him to you. What an idiot. How are you feeling this morning? If you need me to pop round later, I will."

"Josie, none of what happened last night was your fault. He was a creep. I still can't believe that Jack got that violent."

"Amy. This is all my fault. If it weren't for me, you wouldn't have met him. I thought he was a good guy. Every time I've seen him at football, he's always so friendly. He's a bit of flirt, but I had no idea he was like that. The thought of him repulses me now."

The thought of him repulses me now. "It's ok. I still can't believe that people can be that cruel to even come up with this game. Have you heard of this game that Jack was talking about last night?"

"I hadn't, but I asked a couple of the girls who were there last night about it. Basically, it's going around social media at the moment. You don't deserve to be treated like that, and if I ever see him again, we'll be having more than words."

Whilst still talking to Josie, a text from Jack arrives.

"Will I be seeing you at all this week or even this year? xx"

"Jack just texted, so I better go and sort him out. I'll let you know how it goes."

"Ok, babe, well, text me if you need anything. Always here for you."

Jack is always known as a ladies' man, which is why him and Mum have a running joke about which girl he is with that week. He could've got away with telling her that he kissed someone he barely knew as that's what does. I somehow doubt that I would still get the same response from her if I told her what I did last night. I guess we all make mistakes.

"Funnily enough, it never came up; I just played the exhausted card! XX"

I am still upset at Jack due to last night's events but won't give him the silent treatment. I am not THAT annoyed; I'm close, though. After finishing my toast and an enormous mug of tea, I know I need to at least try to attempt to start my day, even if it is nearly the afternoon. As I go through to my wet room, I desperately need to wash my hair as it is rock hard due to the amount of hairspray in it. I can't even get my hairbrush through it. Also, not washing my makeup off last night wasn't the best idea as now I look like a mixture between a panda and a clown, never a good look. The reflection staring back at me has me mortified.

It was lovely of Mum not to mention how I looked when she came in with breakfast. I'm meant to do my physio every morning. I knew the arm over chest exercises would hurt so much this morning, so I decide against it. I'm meant to do two on each side every day. I'm taking today as a rest day; I definitely deserve it.

Whilst finishing getting ready for the day, I receive a text from Jack.

"Hey, we need to talk about what happened last night. Park this afternoon? I'm really sorry xx."

If I invite him over, Mum would be eavesdropping into the whole conversation, so just after two, I walk the short way to the park. My legs are still aching so much that I use my frame to pull them along. It is the beginning of November and freezing. So, I make sure that I have my giant puffer coat on as I know this isn't going to be a quick or easy conversation.

Jack is already there waiting for me to arrive on our usual bench. He slumps on the bench in his grey hoodie and black jeans that he was wearing last night. He looks rough. Jack has his headphones over the top of his hoodie. I put my hand on his shoulder, causing him to jump out of his skin.

As I sit down next to him whilst moving my frame to the side of the bench, I say, "Hey."

He seems very quiet. This side of him is unusual to see. It is as though somebody else is standing in front of me. Although, I am not surprised by his behaviour. He doesn't say anything for a while and seems distracted by the strings of his hoodie. Suddenly, he sits forward and wraps both his arms around my shoulders.

"I'm so sorry." Jack is almost crying, which seems to be a mixture of the hangover, tiredness and realising what he had done last night. As he takes his hood off his head, I can see his black eye and swollen lip.

"Jack! I'm so sorry. Are you ok?" As I was walking to the park, I felt like this was all Jack's fault. Seeing his state makes me realise if I didn't talk to that idiot, none of this would've happened.

"It's ok. You know I'll always protect you even if it means getting beaten up."

"I know you were just trying to protect me, but I didn't want you to get physically hurt. How's your head feeling? Pounding, I take it."

He looks like he is falling asleep. He is definitely a bit delicate.

I'm worried that he is also going to get in trouble because of this. "What did your parents say when you got home?"

"Oh yeah, I should probably tell them. How many did I even have last night? Actually, don't answer that; I think it would just make the situation even worse. I would love to see the state of Jason the morning. What an idiot!" He clears his throat and looks directly into my eyes. "Amy, I'm really sorry about what happened last night. I don't know what came over me. He was a complete knobhead who didn't deserve you and only wanted one thing from you!"

He is right, but I can't just ignore how he had acted. It is so out of character for him and totally uncalled for, even though I know he is only trying to protect me.

"I know, but Jack, I've known you since we were kids. I've seen you in all sorts of different states, some I wish I hadn't. I've never seen you be that violent to anyone. I get that you're protective of me but punching a guy for disrespecting me is not like you at all."

He smiles. "Well, that's because nobody's done that to the

girl that I care the most about. I hear it all the time with the lads from football. They're always talking about how many girls they've pulled this week. That's just the way it is with some lads, unfortunately. You don't deserve to be treated like that all you're not just a number on somebody's list. I don't want people thinking they that can walk all over you."

Jack has always been so caring and protective of me, but in the seven years I've known him, I've never seen him this violent to anyone. "Charming! Jack, I get that I do, but you're the same. Come on, you know it's a running joke how many girls you have on the go at one time."

I can suddenly sense that something was very different. Not in a bad way, in an incredible way. Before I have a chance to work out what it is, it is too late. His lips are pressed against mine. I have to open my eyes to check that this is real but quickly close them again before he notices. So many things are running through my head; this is amazing; am I dreaming? Why now?

He pulls away whilst still holding my hand. "Now you know why I'm so protective of you! I know I may be a real player, but that's only because I didn't want it to ruin our friendship if you didn't feel the same way. So that's why I go from girl to girl because I never want to settle for someone who isn't you! Amy, you're everything I've always wanted; you're funny, smart, and absolutely stunning. So, I guess that idiot was right about one thing." He pauses as I think he's unsure of how I'm going to react. "Seriously, I know I'm pushing well above my standard."

I want him to shut up because I'm not done with that kiss; I decide to go for it. "Jack, we have been friends for years. You could've at least hinted that you wanted something more. It's not like there was someone else." I press my nose up against his.

He lets out a little laugh. "Amy, you don't know how many times I've wanted to tell you all of this. You know I don't have the confidence you show every day, well, at least doing things like this. Seriously it's such an honour to call you my best friend. You empower me to be a better person, because well, I want to make you proud". I was welling up. I never thought I would hear these words from anyone, let alone my best friend.

"Jack, you're amazing. Everything I've always wanted; I care about you so much. I find it funny how I've had two guys call me smart and stunning. Although, I can certainly tell which one of you is saying it from the heart. Just one thing, why me? You know my disabilities can sometimes get in the way, and I don't want them to hold you back. Plus, you're not exactly ugly either you could do so much better."

He pulls me even closer, wraps his arms around me and kisses me once more. "Amy, don't you dare put yourself down just because you've got a disability. You know none of that matters to me. I've never seen you as the girl that uses a walking frame and has seizures. All I see is this incredibly driven and absolutely gorgeous brown-haired, blue-eyed goddess. I will keep saying these things until you believe me."

As we make our way back to mine, both smiling way too much, we stop by the shop. Jack isn't sure where to put his arm as he can't hold my hand whilst we are walking but reaching around my shoulder was a bit awkward. So, he settles for walking behind me and cuddling my waist. All I want to do was watch movies and eat our body weight in chocolate.

As we walk in the door, I can tell that something had happened, and it wasn't good. Mum's eyes are all red and watery. Mum's best friend Amy (who I'm named after) is sitting on the sofa with her arm around Mum. Jack holds onto my hand after I let go of my frame.

"Mum, what's wrong?" She remains silent and just stares down at the ground.

Amy guides me to the sofa. "I think you need to come and sit down." She then turns back to Jack. "Maybe you should go home, Jack; this is a family matter."

I hold onto my frame and stand up quickly. "NO! Something's wrong; I want Jack to be here, let's be honest; he knows everything else anyway."

Amy, Mum, and Jack all stop and look back at me because it is out of the ordinary that I speak like this to my family. Jack sits with me whilst putting his arm around me. It feels a bit awkward but also reassuring.

"We need to tell you something as it's coming out in the

press soon." Mum's words are confusing because "the press" makes it sound like I'm some sort of celebrity. Mum proceeds, "Well, you know how we've always told you that your dad left when you were a baby because he is an alcoholic?"

I nod.

She continues, "That's not exactly the whole story. Your dad is an alcoholic. However, the bit that we purposefully missed out was that whilst being drunk, he actually killed three people, including someone with cerebral palsy and is currently in prison for alcohol-related crimes."

I want to know more, all whilst trying to process what I have already been told.

"Please understand the reason why we didn't tell you this before is for your own protection. No child or anyone wants to know that their dad is a murderer," Mum says.

Instantly, the whole world is spinning in slow motion around me. It feels similar to when I lost my cool with that drama teacher who will remain nameless. I can already sense that this is going to be a lot, a lot worse. I am trying to string a sentence together in my head, but nothing comes out. The only thing that I can feel is Jack's arm moving up and down my back as he is trying to comfort me. It feels like my brain and body are no longer connected, so trying to speak or make a movement seems impossible.

Then I can hear a voice that sounded like it is from a distance. "Amy, Amy, please sweetie, say anything."

"Amy, please say anything." Jack still has hold of my hand

but is looking directly at Mum, extremely concerned.

I take a deep breath and grab hold of Jack's hand so tight, I'm sure I am cutting off his circulation. "Why are you telling me this now?! You did this for my own protection! How am I meant to process this in an hour and then deal with everybody knowing? This is my final year; do you have any idea how stressful it is? Now on top, how am I supposed to deal with this, answers on a postcard, anyone! My father or should I say the man that was responsible for me being conceived. Let's face it; he's done nothing for me my whole life, which has been hard enough to come to terms with. Now I'm supposed just to accept that he has killed someone with a disability! Seriously, Mum, how did you think I was going to react to this! All calm and collected?"

Mum instantly bursts into floods of tears and collapses into a heap on the floor.

"So let me ask you this. How long before everyone else knows?"

Both Amy and Mum look at each other.

Amy says, "I've just got off the phone with a reporter who wanted a statement, but I refused to comment. I'm sorry, but they might track you down as well. I think she said it will be on the news in the next few days."

My teeth were grinding together due to the sheer anger. "What? Because I'm disabled? Because I'm supposedly his daughter? Because my mother kept this from me? Which one? How am I meant to answer any of these?"

Amy kneels down beside Mum, putting her arm around her. "Amy, as we said, it is coming out in the press because the victim's family wants justice." She continues her explanation, but I zone back out.

I look back at Jack. He looks incredibly uncomfortable. I felt awful; not twenty minutes ago, he made me feel like I was on top of the world. Those feelings are a distant memory now. I promptly dash straight to my room, grab my suitcase from the back of my wardrobe and start throwing clothes in. I walk through to the kitchen, pack the medication I need.

"Amy, darling, let's talk about this. I would've told you sooner," Mum says, but I don't want to talk anymore about this.

"I have nothing to say to you!" I promptly turn around and walk straight out of the door. Even through I'm absolutely exhausted, I somehow find the strength to walk of the house and don't look back.

chapter 7

Jenny stops in the hallway as Jack walks through the door carrying my suitcase. Since we're constantly at each other's houses, she doesn't even bat an eyelid.

"Cup of tea, love?" I love how Jenny and I both have the mindset that a cup of tea and gossip can fix even the worst problems. I'm now not so sure that this is going to be the case this time.

"Amy, you, ok?"

I think she can tell that I had been crying due to my puffy and the mascara lines. I start to explain what had happened, but it is still too raw.

Jack says, "Mum, why don't I give you a hand with the teas." I'm so thankful for his quick thinking.

Thankfully none of Jack's nieces and nephews was there, as even though I absolutely adore them, the last thing I need right now is five kids jumping all over me.

Jenny walks back into the living room and sits down beside me "Amy, whatever happens you will always be welcome here and we as a family are always here for you."

My emotions are already fragile, but this has just tipped me over the edge. Having people that accept me not because they have to but because they want to is all I've ever wanted.

Jack's house is like most people's, all the bedrooms and bathrooms are upstairs. This issue didn't even seem to faze him. Before I can even think about a plan for the stairs, he has already picked me up in his arms and start to walk upstairs. Instantly I get the giggles. All I can think about was those scenes from movies where newlyweds go back to their hotel room, and the husband carries their wife over the threshold.

"Don't get any ideas. I've only just said that I like you, one step at a time!" I tease as Jack places me on his bed.

He goes back downstairs to get my suitcase and frame so that if I need the toilet, I can still do it with dignity.

I start to flick through the TV guide whilst he is still downstairs. I turn the volume down as I can hear my name. I can tell Jack is trying not to answer too many questions that his mum is firing at him. I turn the volume down when I hear him starting to walk up the stairs.

"Everything ok?" I ask.

Jack puts my bags down by the bed. "Yeah, just Mum worrying why it looked like you were moving in. I had to tell her what happened at the park and my feelings for you." He kisses me.

When he breaks away, I ask, "What?"

"Nothing, nothing, you've never smiled at me the way you just did. I forget how sweet you can sometimes be. Are the kids over tonight?"

He always knows how to make me laugh in the worst situations. "Well, you make me so happy. We're going to get through the next couple of days together, I promise you. Can I get you anything? Chocolate? Sleeping pill? No, they've got things on at school. So, Mum said they're going to be over this weekend. So, get ready for the questions."

I pull him close and kiss him. I'm just amazed how he's dealing with all of this. It can't be easy hearing that the father of someone you care for is about to be on the national news.

"As I said before, you're all I've ever wanted, and of course, I make you the luckiest girl in the world!"

I laugh at him. Not only are these stupid jokes funny, but they are cute. "I'm so lucky that I've got someone like you to get me through this."

We are halfway through watching *The Greatest Showman,* one of my favourite films, when my phone buzzes. It was a message request. It's Jason.. I already know Jack wants to reply, although it wouldn't be the best idea given how the party ended.

"Hi Amy, I hope you're well. I just wanted to apologise for the way that I behaved at the party. I'm honestly not normally like that. I must've had too many beers or something. I did mean everything I said to you; you are so inspiring, and I think it's amazing what you have achieved. Hope to hear from you soon xx"

I look at Jack because I probably would've gotten together with Jason if it weren't for him.

I think about not replying at all, then send, " *Hi Jason, Um, I'm not sure how you found me, but anyway, you're a bit of a creep. I think you need to learn how to treat women. I don't want to be associated with people like you. I think you need to learn how to actually flirt because, trust me, if that's your technique, no self-respecting woman would want anything to do with you. Your behaviour towards Jack and me was completely unacceptable. I'm so glad that my friends showed me what your true intentions were. Thanks for showing me what my standard is, which by the way, is nowhere near you. I wish you the best of luck but please just leave me alone.*"

I block him and sing my heart out to "This Is Me."

I'm so thankful that I've got incredibly protective friends who always show me my worth and how I only deserve the best.

Jack kisses me on the cheek. "I was never going to tell you what to do but, you know what my opinion is of him. I'm so glad that you've blocked him, he's a total idiot, and I just hope for his sake that I never bump into him. It's funny how

I didn't get an apology."

I just stare him down as he was trying to act like the innocent one in all this.

I really hope that Jack and Jason never meet at a football match. "Really? You're not the angel in this, and he's the devil. You didn't have to punch him in the face. Although, you did gain one thing, though." I stare into his beautiful, piercing blue eyes.

"Oh yeah, what's that?"

"The girl of your dreams."

Jack kissing me is one of the most reassuring feelings in the world.

I dread to think what Jack will actually say or do if we ever see Jason again. "You've shown me already how I should be treated. Which is why I'm not letting you go anywhere."

Today is the day that is going to change everything. All I want to do was stay in bed and skip forward to tomorrow, where there will be another headline that doesn't involve me. My "dad" is going to be on every front cover of every newspaper in the country. His name is already trending on social media. His photo will be on every website that even mentioned the word "news." I wait for Jack to wake up because I don't want to do this on my own, but then I pick up my phone and open the news app; the top story read.

COLD-BLOODED KILLER BROUGHT TO JUSTICE AND WILL SPEND THE REST OF HIS DAYS BEHIND BARS.

As I scroll down to the actual story, I see his name. Kieron, that's all he is to me, a name. He's not a role model, not a parent, just a sperm donor; Mum and Amy did all the hard work. A father is meant to be there for their children, cheer them on and watch them flourish. He hasn't done any of those. Instead, he killed someone with the same disabilities as me. Somehow the press has managed to find out where we live and are camped out on the path by our house. I peer around the curtain for a second. All I can see are people standing there with cameras waiting for us to make an appearance. Although, there isn't going to be a lot that they are going to capture. I know I have a dad, but Mum never really spoke about him.

I already have a family that adores me for me. Why do I need anything else? All I can see was flashing lights; even though the curtains were closed, it's a good thing I don't have photosensitive epilepsy. I always was jealous of my friends who have both parents in their life. When we used to draw our families in primary school, my picture always stood out. Although, that's all I've ever known so it's not like the perfect family and then it got taken away.

I am nervous about stepping out of my house as I was unsure whether they knew I had cerebral palsy. What if they push me over? What if they used my disabilities to write a new story about my family? I'm not sure what reaction they were expecting but sadness was the last emotion on my mind. Why should I be upset about someone who has never done anything for me? He abandoned my mum and doesn't seem to be showing even an ounce of remorse.

Somehow Monday morning has come around quicker than I had hoped. I've been dreading going into school so much so that I have constant knots in my stomach. My life has changed so much in a week; my family had fallen apart. Somehow, I'd fallen in love with my best friend. I'm still unsure how that had happened, but I'm so glad that it did, as it's the one thing that's keeping me going.

I can tell everybody already knows, and walking through the village is extremely difficult. Every house we walk past, we are just stared at. Conversations between pensioners stop; parents who are loading cars ready for the school run just stare. It feels like the rug had been pulled out from under me. What if I lose everything I've worked so hard because of this? Will people treat me differently? Having a disability and connected to a criminal is not a good combination.

Everything I've worked so hard for and the person I've turned out to has now been tarnished by something that's out of my control. Will it if ever be the same? Will people believe me when I say I had nothing to do with it? Do his actions now ruin mine and Mum's reputation?

I can tell everybody at school already knows. The pointing and whispering do the trick. I have to find the strength within me to keep going. This morning's assembly, Mr Perkins is announcing who this year's head boy and head girl would be. So, I can't afford to get distracted by anything, not even this.

Jack has his arm around my shoulder the whole of the way to tutor. It feels like a celebrity had just walked into school as all eyes are focused on me. Everyone crowds me going through the foyer; all I hear is "did you know? Did you know? Did you know?"

"Leave her alone." I'm so grateful for how protective Jack can be in these situations. Everyone suddenly backs off and gives me the space I need.

Making through the tutor room door is such a relief. I've never been happier to see Miss Green. As I make my way to my seat, all eyes are still on me.

"OI! Leave her alone she had nothing to do with it." I'm so thankful that Josie always has my back.

Miss Green makes sure we are all accounted for before escorting us back down to the main hall. "Amy, are you going to be, ok?"

I don't know how to answer because I'm not sure myself. It's so irritating that I have to get the lift up to tutor, sit down for no more than two minutes before going back to where I have just come from. I almost ask whether I can go straight to the main hall, but that goes against everything I stand for, which is just to be treated like everybody else.

The whole year group piles into the main hall. As always, we sit in our tutor groups. I'm away from Jack for the first time since we made it official; it feels like my right arm is missing. Emma and Josie make me sit on the end of the row as they are so sure that I will get appointed as head girl. That's the thing I love about my friends; they have such faith in me, even when I don't have it in myself. I'm incredibly fortunate to be surrounded by amazing people who always pick me up when I need it and shout the loudest cheers when I achieve. They always inspire me to work hard to be the best possible version of myself that I can be.

Mr Perkins makes his way from the back doors of the hall up to the podium. He gathers up his papers and clears his throat. "Good morning. I hope you've all had a fantastic half term and are ready to focus on learning once again."

I look straight at Jack and smile; he winks back at me, immediately sending tingles down my spine.

"As you're all aware, today is a very significant day. We're going to be announcing who will be our head boy and head girl for the remainder of the year."

I take a deep breath and make sure that I have my disappointed but respectful face ready.

:These roles are very prestigious and should be taken with responsibility and pride. We've taken a lot of consideration and deliberation to all of our applicants. We are certain that the students we have selected to fulfil these roles will do an amazing job. We are confident that the six individuals we have selected to make up the team and will all flourish and succeed within their roles."

"So, without further ado, I will be first announcing the head boy. So, it's my privilege and great honour to announce that Josh Pickington."

There is a roar from one side of the hall. No one was able to hear what Mr Perkins says after. Josh is what you would call a real posh boy and uses words such as "chap" or "spiffing" in his everyday language. He isn't a bad person and definitely a good fit, straight-A student, captain of the hockey and football team. I don't really know him; maybe that's a good thing. Josh makes his way up to the front of the hall, collects his badge from Mr Perkins, and shakes his hand.

"Wow! I really wasn't expecting this. I would like to thank Mr Perkins and the rest of the Senior Leadership Team for giving me this honour. I promise I will do the best job I possibly can. For the first time, I'm speechless. So, thank you to everyone who has been on this journey with me. I promise to not let you down." He goes to stand by the rest of the teachers.

Several girls shuffle to the edge of their seats.

"Now the time has come to announce who will be fulfilling our role of head girl. This decision was also incredibly tough. We are very fortunate to have so many strong female role models within this year group, which is why there wasn't an automatic winner. However, after a lot of deliberation, the senior leadership team and I have finally come to a decision".

The suspense is unbearable. I can feel my whole body tensing up; my palms sweat. I'm so focused on Mr Perkins that it could be just the two of us in the hall.

He makes us wait a little bit longer, to add to the suspense. "This young lady is an inspiration to all, every day, she shows others that anything is possible with a bit of grit, hard work, defiance and determination. Life hasn't dealt her the best hand but what she has done with what she's got is truly sensational. I have so much confidence that she will be a fantastic role model and can't wait to see what she achieves while being in this role."

There's a buzz building up around the hall.

"So, it's my great honour and privilege to congratulate Amy Webb as our new head girl!"

Everything becomes slow motion. Nothing feels real. It almost sounded like Mr Perkins said my name. How can that be? Me! The girl who has cerebral palsy and epilepsy has been named as the new head girl? There has got to be some kind of mistake.

Everyone jumps up and looks in my direction as I stand and get into my frame. I walk along the aisle that not ten minutes ago, I was mocking Mr Perkins for. I didn't have time to check that I look ok. What if my hair is a mess? What if I have a bat hanging out of the cave? It is almost as if I was walking on air. Before I know it, I am at the front of the school hall. Mr Perkins attaches my new, red, head girl badge to my jumper and shakes my hand whilst the school photographer captured the moment. The applause is so loud that I blink.

"Hang on!" someone yells.

There is a gasp from the rest of the year group.

Hannah, my arch-nemesis continues, "Sir, how can you give the title of head girl to someone whose father is in prison for being a murder and is in a walking frame? Is she even capable of being head girl? This has to be some kind of mistake!"

The whole of the year group gasps.

Hannah couldn't just let me have this moment without butting in. Since year seven, when I was picked to be the student council representative, we have never seen eye to eye. I can see she's gearing up to go again.

"How can you make someone who is special head girl?" she asks.

I'm shocked she said this, but I'm ready to take her down.

Mr Perkins straight away asks Miss Green, our tutor, to escort Hannah out of the hall immediately. I can tell that he's furious and so is the rest of the year group. Many voices are building up throughout the hall. Somehow, a red-faced Mr Perkins manages to calm himself. "That's enough, year 13! Amy, the floor is yours."

He steps aside as I move forward to the podium. Given that I didn't actually think I would win and am still in a state of shock, I have to make it seem like I'm confident and well put together, I have to totally WING THIS!

Given everything that is going on with my sperm donor, all eyes are on me. I clear my throat and take a deep breath.

"I would first off like to thank the senior leadership team for giving me this fantastic opportunity. I promise I will do my very best not to let you down. I'm going, to be honest, I will make mistakes because we all do, but I will try and learn from each mistake. I would also like to thank everyone who ever doubted me."

Several teachers and students look puzzled.

"Believe it or not, you've helped me to become stronger, wiser, and more resilient. Anyone who ever told me I couldn't do something; I would just do it to prove them wrong. I'm also well aware that I'm the first head girl who has a disability, so I hope to be a role model for others to show that anything is possible. In terms of my promise to you as your new head girl," how weird to say that, "I promise that I will do my best to listen to your opinion and always put your ideas forward. Oh, one last thing, I'm well aware of what had just come out in the press even before a certain someone had brought it up." I know not mentioning the story would be even worse. "So, I will say this, family doesn't always mean the people who we are related to by blood. Family are those individuals in each of our lives that elevate us at our best and soothe us at our worst. Come on, year thirteen, let's make great people out of ourselves and do it for us!"

The sheer volume of applause that echoes through the hall causes me to tear up. After the assembly, Mr Perkins asks Josh and I to see him in his office.

I hold onto my frame for dear life whilst walking out of

the assembly hall. How embarrassing would it be to fall over now! As I make my way out of the foyer and towards Mr Perkins's office, several teachers and students look at me in disbelief like there is some sort of mistake.

Josh is already there and sitting on one of the comfy chairs outside the office. Usually, you will find the kids that have been kicked out of lessons here. We both hear Mr Perkins call for us to "come in" from where he is inside the office. Josh ushers me to go first, much to my surprise. From what I've heard about him, he can apparently be very selfish and incredibly self-centred.

Mr Perkins stands up from his chair and goes to close the door behind us. I feel terrible because of my frame means he has to squeeze past. "Congratulations to the both of you. As I said in the assembly, it was a very tough decision, but your personalities definitely stood out, and I look forward to you both representing the school this year."

He then explains our key roles, such as being good representatives of the school's ethos, attending school events, being a role model for younger students, and ensuring that the other prefects are fulfilling their duties correctly.

We have quite a lengthy meeting explaining what we plan to do with our new roles. I'm adamant about making sure that the school is more diverse and inclusive for all students. I know I need to highlight the importance of ensuring that every student, no matter what their abilities or disabilities, is given equal access and opportunities to achieve their full potential.

I then explain that I want to reintroduce a student council whereby anyone can come to meetings and voice their opinions about what needs to be changed within the school. Unfortunately, the organisation of these meetings has been non-existent over the past few years.

After spending an hour in a relatively small stuffy office, the meeting has finally come to an end. Although, whilst Mr Perkins is wrapping up, he says that he needs to see me for a minute before I go to my lesson, which is maths, so I didn't have a problem with this at all. Josh lets himself out of the office; I wait until the door had closed and then turn back around to face Mr Perkins.

"Amy, I'm very proud that you are our head girl, and you definitely deserve it after all your hard work. I can assure you that you have my full confidence and know you will do an amazing job. I can only apologise for Hannah's outburst. I want to assure you that the situation will be dealt with appropriately. However, I do have a question to ask you?"

He takes a big gulp of water. "So, I didn't know how to bring this up because I understand it's a very sensitive subject, and my thoughts go out to you and your family. That aside, I can't ignore the news that broke out last night. Therefore, I need to know from you truthfully did you know anything about the incident beforehand?"

I knew this would come up at some point which is why I have my answer fully prepared. "Sir, I knew about an hour before the news broke out. Growing up, I did always wonder about where and who my dad was. My mum didn't really say much, just that we couldn't see him, so I just had to accept that. I'm still trying to process it all myself. As you can imagine, it's a lot for anyone to take in, in such a short amount of time. I assure you, if I knew about the situation beforehand, my reaction would've been very different."

He smiles, which I take as reassurance. "Well, I appreciate that. However, the headteacher has told me to tell you that if anything does come up that contradicts your story, then your position may be in jeopardy."

I can't believe this! Something that is totally out of my control could potentially get in the way of my achievements.

I smile back at him. "I promise that I won't let you down." Once again, I have to prove myself. Now the stakes are severe.

Mr Perkins walks with me out of his office and then turns to face me.

"I look forward to seeing what you come up with. Many congratulations once again, Amy." He shakes my hand and proceeds back into his office.

"Baby, baby, wait up!" Jack is running down the corridor to catch up with me. I'm confused about why he's not in his lesson. He picks me up and kisses me. "I'm so bloody proud of you. I knew you could do it."

Mr Perkins suddenly appears in his office doorway. "Jack, why aren't you in lesson? I believe you should be in history with Mr Hornby?" Unfortunately, this isn't the first time Jack has got into trouble for not being in lesson.

"Umm, I'm so sorry, sir, but I wanted to see my girl," he says whilst winking at me, "as soon as I could. I'm so proud of her."

I'm unsure whether or not Jack was about to get yet another detention.

"Alright, Jack, I will let you off this one time given the circumstances, but I don't want to see you rooming the corridors again, you hear me, young man?" Mr Perkins says.

Jack nods and grabs my hand so we can race off to our lessons.

I enter my maths lesson to a round of applause, which is a very welcoming change to just being ignored. Mrs Evans settles everyone down and congratulates me on the way to my seat. She then carries on with the lesson about our exam and the skills we need to know to get a good grade. I usually don't pay attention in maths because, typically, Mrs Evans doesn't really support those students who she thinks aren't going to get good grades. It's amazing how one change can have such an impact; it also highlights how bad her teaching practice was beforehand.

I always find that having cerebral palsy causes teachers to react to how they're meant to teach me in several different ways. Some just outright ignore me because they don't see the point of teaching me. Some talk to me really slowly like I'm an idiot. Unfortunately, very few actually treat me like any other student or even person. Today, Mrs Evans makes sure that she includes me in all discussions, which shows how bad her teaching practice was before this. I make a note of this to raise this issue with Mr Perkins in our next meeting.

Jack doesn't let go of my hand the whole of the bus journey home; I think he missed me. Due to my new commitments, I've hardly seen him all day. However, being the understanding boyfriend he is, he doesn't really mind or at least that's what he told me. He doesn't take his arm from around my shoulder until we walk through his front door. Even though it had only been a couple of days, I'm getting used to living with him. I'm so grateful to Jack's parents, Jenny, and Mark, for taking me in. They're both so understanding and make me instantly feel at home. Jenny ensured that all my medications are in a place where I can find it and even helps me with my physio. She also offered to pick up my prescription when it's ready, so I don't have to rush out of school to get there before the pharmacy closed.

As we walk in the front door, all of the kids are in the living room. Mia and Beth are getting on with their homework.

I ask, "How did you get on today, Beth? Year seven is not easy; I remember it well and am glad that I never had to repeat it."

She looks up from her phone. "Yeah, it was fine, pretty boring, to be honest." She immediately glances back at her phone.

She looks up again and says, "Amy, now that you're head girl, which I'm so proud of you for getting, and you deserve it."

None of Jack's nieces and nephews are only ever this nice to me when they want something. One second later she asks, "Does this mean you can get us out of having detentions?"

"Beth, how have you already got a detention? I take it your dad doesn't know about this? Which is why you're here?"

She just looks down at the ground. "No, they don't. I would really appreciate Uncle Jack if you didn't tell him?"

Jack is such a pushover with all the kids that they use this to their advantage.

Jack carries me up the stairs; this time, a fireman lift sends me into fits of laughter. We get comfy in his room and remove my splints which is such a relief. I spread out all of my books on his bed as I want to keep on top of my workload this year. Jack, on the other hand, is watching TV even though I'm sure he has homework as well. Just as I am getting focused on my first assignment, my phone goes off. I had it off at school, which is probably for the best. It is from Mum. Due to the betrayal, I almost don't read but, she's hurting a lot right now. So, me being angry with her isn't going to help the situation.

"The story will be on the 6 o'clock news. Sorry, my lovely but I needed to let you know. I hope you had a good day.

I'm sorry, proud of you, Mum xx"

I am a bit confused about how she knew about me getting head girl. Jack must have let her know as he knew I wasn't going to tell her. I'm glad that she had given me some warning. As the story is airing tonight, thankfully I'd avoided speaking to the press; what a relief.

"Babe, we need to watch the news tonight. They're going to air the story," I say.

"How do you feel about it, baby? I know we've spoken about it a lot, but you know you can tell me anything and I promise it won't go any further unless you want it too."

"I'm not sure," I admit.

I've spent so much time trying to process the story, and apart from my angry outburst to Mum and Amy, I haven't really shown much emotion. I think it would've been different if he was involved in my life. Unfortunately for him, he was someone I just knew the name of; I've actually learnt more about him over the past day than I have in seventeen years. The only thing that does annoy me is that Mum has kept it from me this whole time. Now suddenly everything has blown up.

I decide it would be best to have a conversation with Jenny and Mark about the news because I'm very aware of how much stress it could put on the whole family. Thankfully, Jack's oldest is over so he watches the kids whilst we head into the dining room.

"Ok where do I start?" I ask as Jack holds my hand. "I

just want to check with you both that you're still ok with me being here. I'm so thankful for everything you've done for me already but honestly, I don't know how people in the village are going to react to this. I just don't want this family getting hurt when you had nothing to do with it."

I prepare myself for the worst.

Jenny grabs both my hands. "Amy, none of this is your fault. I see you as another daughter and I promise you, you will always be welcome in this home."

Tears start to fall down my face.

chapter 8

Finally, the time has come for the whole nation to find out who my father is and the senseless crime he has committed. Jack turns on the TV and shuts his bedroom door; I only want him with me. As he kisses me, he says, "Whatever happens, I'll be here for you. I love you, baby." I pick up the remote and flicked it on.

"Good evening and welcome to the *News at 6*." A blonde middle-aged woman stands with a script in her right hand in front of a large screen. She wears a turquoise blouse and a black pencil skirt. "Our main headlines this evening." The intense music kicks in. "Justice is finally brought to the family who has been fighting for years after their daughter was brutally killed fourteen years ago."

My sperm donor's photo shoots up onscreen. My heart sinks; this is real, this is now, and this is my life. I hold onto

Jack tighter than I ever have before and take a deep breath.

The reporter then turns to face a different camera within the studio. "A very good evening to you. Today, justice has been brought to the Jones family, after a gruelling fourteen-year wait. Andrew and Kelly Jones, whose daughter Monique was brutally killed on a late September evening in 2002, finally understand the truth behind their daughter's death. Monique Jones was walking home at around 11 p.m. on a late September evening after attending a friend's house party. She was last seen walking a few streets away from her house. Her body was found the following morning abandoned in a nearby forest. Two other bodies were discovered at the scene, and after thoroughly searching the crime scene, a wheelchair was also found.

"Due to the condition in which the bodies were found in, police could not identify them at the scene. Monique's body had several gunshot wounds, and the attacker was likely shooting to kill. Monique's family has never given up hope and have continued to fight for answers and justice for their daughter. Today, forty-eight-year-old Michael Webb has been found guilty of this brutal killing. Mr Webb is currently serving time for substance abuse unrelated to this offence at HMP Hazelton and is still adamantly stating he is not guilty. Mr Webb denied the charges at the time of the crime. After the testimony that a representative of the family gave in court today, there is now clear evidence that Mr Webb is guilty and will serve his sentence at the same prison. We are still unsure as to why Monique and the of other two bodies were victims of this crime.

"Earlier this afternoon, her family made a statement saying she was a wonderful, funny, and caring daughter who really made the most out of life. She was training to become a doctor; many of her colleagues have taken to social media throughout the day. One of them stating that she was confident and inspiring. She always had time for anyone and everyone, no matter how busy she was. Mr Webb has been convicted and will now face a life sentence without parole."

At this point, I have to turn off the TV; I can't bear to hear anymore. That is it; everyone now knows the secret that Mum has kept to herself for years; there is no going back now. Jack still has his arm around me; he remains silent. I lean on his stomach and push myself up. I look straight at him. "Jack, in all seriousness, do you still love me?"

Shock shifts through his handsome face. "Amy, seriously? That's not you. You're nothing like him; you're kind, funny and caring. Family, we can't change even if it means we have to accept things that we don't want to. It's his loss that he hasn't got to see his inspiring daughter turn into a strong, empowering woman. If anything, I love you even more because you wanted me to be with you when you watched this."

"Jack, are you sure? There's so much you've had to take on being with me, and now this I just want to make sure that you're ok as well? I sometimes wonder whether or not

I'm holding you back."

He looks directly into my eyes, pulls me closer and kisses me on the forehead. "Babe, that's exactly why I love you; even in situations like this where you have every right to be a little bit selfish, you still worry about me. I can promise you that you don't have to ever worry about me disappearing; you're everything to me. I wouldn't change you for anything even though you drive me crazy sometimes. I wouldn't have you any other way. Every day I wake up feeling like the luckiest man in the world because I have the honour of calling you my girlfriend. You have no idea how much you've changed me since we've been together. You know I've never really been a boffin at school, and only do the bare minimum to get by. Well, now that I'm dating the head girl, I've definitely felt the pressure to focus more. My teachers are hardly saying my name in lessons which I think is scaring them a bit."

Whilst pulling me even closer, I wrap my arm around his stomach and whisper in his ear, "I love you so much."

"However, there is one thing that I think you should do."

"Ring, mum?"

He smiles at me.

"Just check that she's ok and I'll order us a takeaway, pizza?"

As if I would order anything else. He kisses me and then walks out of the room to phone the pizza place. I sit up from the bed and stretch my legs as they have tensed up. I hold the phone to my ear; there are only two rings before I hear her familiar voice.

"Hello darling, I guess you saw the news?"

I take a deep breath. "Yeah, I did. How are you doing?"

Mum is silent for a moment. I think she's surprised that I'm even asking after her, given the amount of information she has thrown at me lately.

By the sound of her voice, I can tell she is trying to hold back the tears. "Oh, thanks darling, yeah, I'm ok. I mean, do I wish the person that I fell in love with all those years ago didn't turn out to be a murderer? Of course, I do." She pauses.

"Mum, he doesn't define us, and he never will. We had no control over what he did. Now it's out there; we can get on with our lives without the fear of the story dropping at any time. He's done the crime, so now he has to do the time."

She knows that I'm right; by the sound of it, a weight has been lifted off her shoulders. I want to see her to show her that I'm not angry at her at all because truthfully, I was going to find out one day she was trying to protect me. "However, I can promise you one thing."

"What's that, darling? I'm so proud of how you're dealing with this. You really are such a strong, independent young women."

"I won't ask you about him again. I've now learnt; the less I know, the better. I tell you what, how about Jack and I pop round in a bit?"

"Oh sweetie, that would be lovely. I'll have the kettle on ready, love you, darling."

I know I need to show that I'm not mad at her. She's in no way to blame for what my sperm donor did. I've now learnt that I don't need to go looking for a family, when I already have everything, I could possibly need.

By the time I get off the phone, the pizza has arrived. Jack orders my favourite cheese and ham with extra cheese on top. We sit on Jack's bed, both tucking in, when Harry, Jack's youngest nephew, pops his head around the door. "Amy? Please, can I have a slice? I'll be your best friend forever!" It's adorable how he had asked.

"You'll have to check with your uncle first." I look back at Jack; he doesn't look amused.

"Nope, go away, because if I give you a bit, then everyone else will want a slice, and then they will be none left for us. Anyway, this is a treat for Amy."

Harry immediately runs out of the room, slamming the door after him.

"He'll get over it."

I don't know how, but Jack seems to be immune to the whole situation. However, when you have three nephews and two nieces all asking for things all the time, it probably gets annoying after a while. I often give in to them; it's almost impossible to say no to their cute faces.

After dinner and walking all the kids home, Jack and I

pop round to mine.

"Mum, I'm home," I say, walking through the front door.

Over the years, Mum has been good at hiding her pain and putting on a strong face. I know straight away she has been crying. Her eyes are all puffy; mascara is streaming down her face. I push my frame over to her as fast as I can and immediately wrapped my arms around her. "It's ok, we're both here for you now."

Jack sits on the other side of Mum.

She takes a deep breath to calm herself. "Do you think you can forgive me?"

"Forgive you for what? Mum, nothing that has happened is your fault. I think it's incredible that you managed to have the strength to raise me on your own, considering you had no idea how my life was going to pan out."

"Sweetie, I had no choice. You kept me going and were such a bundle of joy. I'm so sorry that I didn't tell you sooner, it's I didn't know how." It is hard to understand her as she is sobbing at the same time. "I just didn't want to say, and to be honest, I only knew what your father told me before he went on the run."

I feel awful for treating her so poorly when she told me, all she wanted to do was prepare me.

"Mum, it's ok, it's not your fault," I say whilst rubbing her back, trying to console her.

Jack and I are both looking at each other, unsure what we are meant to say or do. Mum leans over with her head in her hands. After several minutes she sits up. It is almost like Jack and I see the weight being lifted that she has been carrying for so long all by herself.

A few days later, for the first time, I think about using the epilepsy card as I am dreading the looks, I will get when I go back to school. However, this is not me and nor will ever be; my disability pushes me forwards instead of holding me back. The mornings have gone from the start of the autumn cool, clean air to the depressing wet mornings of winter. I never look forward to the winters as my muscles can seize up, causing enormous amounts of pain. The only thing that helps them to relax is a long, hot bubble bath. Whilst popping home over the weekend as I needed some time away, I make sure to pick up my fluffy winter coat that feels like the softest blanket wrapped around me.

I don't want to move all my stuff into Jack's as my plan isn't to move in with him permanently. I feel badly that I am leaving Mum all by herself to deal with this. I just hope that Amy has been popping in to support her. Unfortunately, she did hide all of this from me and the way that I've had to find out hasn't been easy. I'm sure when all this has blown over, and there's a different story in the news, I'll move back home.

I arrive at school early as I need to have a meeting with Mr Perkins to discuss issues that I wanted to raise this term. As I am making my way up the school drive, my phone buzzed.

"Good morning, darling, hope today goes ok. I'm still sorry for this whole situation even if you say it wasn't my fault love you loads, my amazing inspirational daughter. Mum xxx."

I'm so glad that she still being so supportive; she really is a real-life superhero. If I was in her position and my daughter spoke to me the way I spoke to her the other day, I'm sure my response would be very different. By the time I've finally arrived at school, I only had five minutes to get to Mr Perkins's office.

He is already there. "Amy, thanks for coming into school early to have this meeting. I promise I won't keep you long." He gestures for me to take a seat opposite him. "I was wondering what your proposed motions are for change whilst you're the school's head girl?"

I suddenly draw the biggest smile possible, reach inside to grab my sparkly folder with all my proposed motions because obviously, I have this prepared. "Well, sir, thank you for asking. I believe that one of the big stories in the media at the moment, aside from my sperm donor," he instantly smiles, "is mental health. I think that as a school, we should be more productive about making sure that if any students need support, they know where to go and who they can talk to. After all, we have a school nurse to look after our physical health. Therefore, we should also have a service that takes care of our mental health as well. This is so that all students can get the best from their education, whilst still meeting all their needs, whether they are physical or mental.

Mr Perkins, I'm not sure if you were aware, but just this year, only 12.6 percent of all students in secondary school, including those in sixth form, have had to have some kind of support with their mental health."

He sits back in his chair whilst nodding his head as if he agreed. I carried on "as we are both aware that my personal life outside of school is a bit rocky at the moment. Hence, I want to use this experience to help others who may not be willing to come forward on their own and ask for support."

Mr Perkins continues to smile at me. "Well, that's incredibly noble of you, Amy. I must say there aren't many individuals I know that would use their experiences to help others, so thank you for that. I find your whole attitude so positive and refreshing. I'm still unsure how you can keep this upbeat all the time. See, this is why we made you our head girl, you're such an inspirational role model; I hope that many students adopt your attitude. You're absolutely right about this issue. I think some members of staff don't take it seriously. For many years, people were told to keep quiet about having any sort of mental health issue. Which is why, I think, some teachers don't talk about it with students. I think it would also be nice to see teachers being more open about their own struggles. So, thank you for addressing this. It's something that I will raise within the next staff meeting." He pauses for a moment, fingers steepled on his desk. "So, Amy, how do you think you'll achieve this?"

I already have it all planned out as I knew he would ask

this. "Well, sir, I find that the most effective way of getting to students is by using social media to its advantage. I did think about doing a focus group. However, I know that some individuals may not want to come to it and share their issues. Therefore, using social media will mean that individuals who want to remain anonymous when asking for support they can do so without judgment. I've had my fair share of judgment from both students and teachers due to my disabilities. So, I think it's time to support those who need it and not just brush it under the carpet. Also, if we can show as a school that we are taking all students well being seriously, then I'm sure it will be a positive for our next OFSTED report. As we both know, being a teenager can be tough even on the strongest of students. So, it's important that we change attitudes and just like the saying goes, it's ok to not be ok."

After fourteen years of being in education, you soon learn that mentioning the word OFSTED sparks fear in teachers immediately. He leans forward in his chair. "That's fine, Amy, just make sure that you're complying with all relevant policies and procedures. I do really admire you for continuing to make a difference to the lives of those around you."

I had already read all the relevant ones before having this meeting with him. I am almost about to ask what Josh's proposed plans are. However, I didn't want to make it look like it is a competition.

"Thanks, sir, the only thing I will need is an email address that I can have access to, and students can reach me on. I will create social media accounts that are completely separate from my personal ones. I will also make sure that they are only used for this purpose. Oh, also, if possible, I need access to either a laptop or computer for one hour a week, please?"

He agrees to both of these requests. He says that he will sort this out and have the materials I need by the end of the day. Just then, the bell rings for the first lesson.

As I quickly make my way to English with Mr Roberts; instead of sitting at his desk, he is in the doorway. I am pretty sure I am in trouble, which is why I speed up my walking. This can be pretty risky when you use a walking frame. "I'm sorry, sir. Mr Perkins wanted to see me."

He steps inside the room whilst still smiling.

"Oh, don't worry, Amy. I knew where you were. I actually have something for you. I know you're not living at home at the moment, so your mum sent this to the school."

I am slightly confused about several things; why am I getting things sent to the school? Two, why didn't Mr Perkins give it to me in the meeting that we just had? I sit down in my usual seat and began to tear open the envelope.

> *Dear Miss Webb,*
>
> *I hope this letter finds you well. I am writing to inform you that you have been invited to attend one of our audition days that will be held on the 22nd of January. Within this audition, we will be looking for*

outstanding levels of talent and ambition. The audition itself will be free of charge. However, we ask applicants to cover the costs of their travel arrangements to and from the audition.

Please note that feedback will not be given after your audition. This is due to the sheer number of applicants. If you require any additional support in order for you to attend the audition, please do not hesitate to contact us prior to the date stated above. We will do our very best to meet these requirements. Please be prepared that sometimes we are unable to facilitate these requirements.

RADA is always proud to invite anyone to audition, we very much pride ourselves on being inclusive and diverse. We always do our best to support those with additional needs not just at the audition process but throughout their whole time at RADA. We will always encourage applicants to declare any additional needs that they may have.

The audition itself will be in stages and will be explained to you by one of the performing arts coaches at the time of your arrival. However, one of the stages will be a performance of your chosen Shakespeare monologue. Therefore, we do ask that you prepare this ahead of the audition.

Please could you email us back at your earliest convivence to state whether or not you would be available on this date. If you have any questions for us prior to the audition, please do not hesitate to contact us.

I very much look forward to hearing from you soon. Once again, many congratulations on getting this far.

Yours Sincerely,
Edward Kemp
Director of RADA

I reread the letter several times to make sure that I'm not dreaming.

Mr Roberts smiles back at me. "Congratulations, Amy. You've worked so hard for this."

Nerves and excitement pulse through my veins.

After a few minutes, I suddenly display a smile so big that my cheeks start to hurt. "This has to be kind of mistake."

"Well, Amy, considering everything that's going on with your family at the moment, we thought it was best that you opened it here. You definitely deserve this; I think I can say on behalf of the whole school we are rooting for you."

All I want to do was ring Mum and see Jack. "Sir, I know we're not meant to use our phones—"

"Amy, you can use the phone in my office. Oh, and Jack's on his way down." He smiles at me in the way that adults do when they know about your dating lives, but I really could care less at this point. He shuts the behind him so that I can have some privacy.

"Good morning, Tilly's Café. How can I help you?"

"Hi Mum, it's me."

Before I can explain why I was ringing, she says, "Is everything alright, darling? Why aren't you in a lesson? Do you need me to come and get you?" I can imagine Mum getting her coat and trying to find her car key.

I try to interrupt her a few times between these questions. "Mum, Mum, MUM!" She stops talking, and I say, "Everything's fine, I'm in Mr Robert's office. I've received a letter from RADA."

Mum's voice suddenly becomes very intense. "And?"

I leave her waiting for a minute just to add to the suspense. after all, I'm going to be a drama student. Well, hopefully.

"I got an audition!" This is the first time that I've actually said it out loud, and here comes the water works.

"Oh, Amy! That's AMAZING! I'm so proud of you, sweetheart. I knew that they would want to see you because of your amazing talent."

I am still in disbelief; saying it out loud still doesn't make it seem even a tiny bit real.

After I get off the phone from Mum, I turn around and see Jack leaning up against Mr Robert's door. He immediately runs to me and throws me up in the air like I am a feather. "Well done, baby!"

He kisses me and squeezes me tight. His reaction is so sweet and perfect. It is all I need to know that this is real. Whilst Jack still has his arms wrapped around my waist, Mr Roberts clears his throat. We both look at him.

"I'm so sorry, sir, I'm just so proud of this one," Jacks says whilst grabbing both my arms and giving the biggest smile I have ever seen from him.

"It's fine; I definitely miss being young and in love. Although married life is great as well, believe me!" he says this in such a tone, it's as if his wife is listening in on the conversation.

We both laugh. You never imagined teachers being young and doing all the stupid stuff we get up to now.

Jack walks with me to my next lesson and stops outside the door looked at me. "I'm so proud of you, Amy. I love you. We've now got two reasons to celebrate on Saturday, and I can't wait!"

chapter 9

With Christmas just around the corner, there is certainly a buzz around school. Being head girl, I still have a long to-do list before I can enjoy the festivities. Every day I am stumbling through the door, exhausted. I know I have to be extremely careful as tiredness is one of the main causes of my seizures. Being so busy also means that I hardly see Jack the whole week that leads up to the end of term. On top of this, I only have less than a month to go until my RADA audition. I can't afford to be ill!

"Hey babe, what are we actually doing for your birthday on Saturday?" Jack asks, spread out on his bed, pretending to get on with his coursework.

Given how much Jack has already done for me this year, I don't really want him to think that he needs to put in loads of effort.

"Oh, sweetie, don't worry about doing anything. You have already done so much for me this year. Let's just get a takeaway or something and watch a film, *The Greatest Showman*?"

He seems almost outraged by this suggestion. "No!"

I jump out of my skin.

"This is the first birthday we've had together as a couple; if I don't do anything, then you're never going to let me forget it; I know what you're like. Then when we're married and get into an argument; this will be one of the things you bring up. Plus, when you love someone, all you want to do is spoil them," he says.

He does have a point, but I still feel awful for even suggesting anything. "Ok babe, what do you have in mind? Wait, hang on, you've thought about that?"

"Well, how about I take my beautiful, incredible girlfriend out for a romantic dinner? I was thinking Nando's?" He always treats me to the nicer places, well, on a seventeen-year-old's budget. "After all, you deserve the best. Of course, I do, Amy; you're all I've ever wanted." He locks his fingers into mine and kisses me.

"Well, mister, you sure do know how to treat your lady."

I sometimes forget how sweet Jack can be when he wants to be. He's definitely a keeper.

"Well, what can I say after all these years of being a player, now I've got the most incredible girlfriend who pushes me to be a better person. I don't know what I would do if I lost you." He kisses me on the forehead.

"Well, baby, you don't have to worry about that. Just hearing you talk about our future is everything I've ever wanted to hear. I love you so much."

It is the day of my birthday; I get breakfast in bed, complimentary of Jack and had a mountain of presents. He spoils me with a Pandora bracelet and a charm that has "forever and always" on it. Jack has sent me out for the whole day before we go out for dinner in the evening. Josie, Emma, and I end up getting our nails done. I decide to go for a bright red colour with glitter accents, something to get me in the mood. Jack also booked for me to have my hair done at one of those posh salons. I send him a message.

"Hey babe, Josie's invited me over for a drink. I don't think I'll be long. I'll walk back to yours in plenty of time for dinner, hope this is ok love you lots. xx."

Growing up, Mum could never afford to pay for haircuts; she either did it herself or would get Amy to do it. I always have fond memories of when she would get a bit too excited and ended up cutting off way more than she wanted to. We would have music pumping out throughout the house to get her in the mood. Generally, it was either Blondie or Fleetwood Mac. Mum is such an 80s fan. To make things worse, when she did try and even it out, it just looked worse. I managed to find the funny side of it and just said to her, "Oh well, at least now I have a haircut to match my balance and coordination."

After feeling rather pampered, Josie suggests that we get ready at hers. I find this strange as we are only going to Nando's; it's not like I need to get dressed up. I tell Jack.

Instantly I saw the three little dots. *"Of course, I don't mind! Go have fun, and I'll be seeing your beautiful face soon. Love you, my gorgeous girl xx."*

It is also weird that Josie is getting ready to go out as well. "So, where are you off to tonight then?"

She almost looks stunned that I asked this question.

"Oh, I'm eh, going to an um party." Josie's behaviour is very odd. She never has a problem with getting her words out. Usually, it's the complete opposite; getting her to shut up is always the challenge. "Right Am's, you ready?"

As Josie's is getting her bag ready and grabbing her keys and I am about to text Jack to see where he is, there's a knock at the door.

"Are you ready, beautiful?" Jack stands at the doorway, looking rather dapper in a dark blue suit. He makes sure that I go into Jenny's car safely before getting into the other side of the car.

"Happy Birthday, you look beautiful," Jenny says as she looks at me through the rearview mirror.

"Um, babe, aren't you a little overdressed for Nando's?" I ask.

"I don't care; it's your birthday, so I needed to make an effort. Although do you mind if we take a slight detour?"

At this point, I'm even more confused.

"Mum, you know the address." He kisses me and smiles. "Happy Birthday, beautiful."

For some reason, we are heading the complete opposite way to the town centre. We were actually heading to his house. "Oh yeah, I didn't tell you, I forgot my phone, so we're just going to swing by mine, and then we'll head out for dinner."

As we arrived at his, he says, "Oh yeah, I've actually got something for you inside and don't really want to take it to the restaurant with us. You know how bad my memory is." He comes around to my side with my frame.

"Ok? I mean, I'm not sure why you can't give it to me later or tomorrow."

Jack holds my hand and leads me down his front path whilst my other hand is clenching my frame as tightly as possible so that I didn't fall over.

Jack opens the door and people bellow, "SURPRISE!! HAPPY BIRTHDAY, AMY!!"

My whole body tenses up. I'm shocked that everyone I love is standing right in front of me.

I immediately look back at Jack. "So, this is why you've been acting so weird?"

He puts his arms around my waist and kisses my head. "This is what you deserve, happy birthday, beautiful!"

As I walk into his front room, all I can see is a sea of people who I absolutely adore and who have been there for me through my ups and downs. Somehow Jack managed to track down Mum's old friends, Shaun and Lauren. I've always called them the uncle and auntie that I've never had. Well, apart from Amy. Throughout my whole life, they've never treated me any differently, despite my disabilities. When Shaun picks me up, I instantly am transported to my seven-year-old self, drinking lemonade and eating chocolate digestive biscuits. Shaun and Lauren have always been there when I've needed them most. Even though they now live for hours away, I know they would never any harm done to Mum or me.

"Hello, Trouble! Happy birthday; how are you doing?" Shaun started calling me Trouble eleven years ago. Sometimes nicknames never disappear. He shakes Jack's hand. "Hey mate, it's good to finally meet you, Amy's told me so much about you."

"Amy, you've done well for yourself. Do I hear wedding bells?" That's what I love about Lauren; she always says it as it is.

"Slow down. One thing at a time. It's taken this one," I say whilst looking at Jack, "nearly seven years to realise that he actually likes me more than a friend."

I know this will set Lauren off.

"Oh, really, Jack? Why has it taken you so long to admit your feelings for this inspirational girl?" She puts her arm around me.

Jack is stumped for words. "Can I get you two a drink?"

Jack would rather run away than have the awkward conversation.

Both Shaun and Lauren just look at each other and smile. "I like him; seems like someone I can wind up," Shaun says as he squeezes me tight.

"So, is your mum here? How is she with everything?" Lauren is scanning the room for her.

I was waiting for the story to come up. I don't know what to say as I don't want to come across as a spoilt brat who left her mum to deal with one of the worse situations she's ever been in all by herself.

"No, unfortunately, Mum's not here. I've temporally moved into here just while everything settles down."

Lauren nods her head as if we have just finished the conversation telepathically.

The whole evening is incredible; Jack has even organised a special rainbow birthday cake, which is beautiful. I always find it so awkward when people sing happy birthday; who are you meant to look at? What are you meant to do? I'm so glad when it's over.

chapter 10

Jack's parents have a Christmas party the weekend before the end of term, and it definitely gets me in the festive spirit. During the holidays, Mum and I don't put much effort in as it's only the two of us. Their house is beautifully decorated with an enormous tree in their front room with silver and white baubles covering it; the tree is also lit up with those cute multi-coloured twinkly lights. Decorations also cover every inch of their house with tinsel on the bookshelves, a wreath on the front door and smaller Christmas trees in nearly every other room. They even have lights up on the front of their house. I always have fond memories of Mum and I driving around the local neighbourhoods, looking at all the different colours, this never fails to get me in the festive mood. The best house I've ever seen is when we went down to the coast one year and the whole nativity scene was displayed on someone's front lawn. It looked magical.

Mr Perkins asks me to attend the school's Christmas fair to have a chance to speak to some of the governors who I have not met yet. Even though they don't have any authority over the school's day-to-day running, they do have control over the big decisions at the school, like the Year Thirteen prom, which is why it was essential for me to make an excellent first impression.

As I walk into the main hall, I can hear the familiar Christmas carols we all learnt in primary school, such as "Silent Night" and "Away in a Manger." The school's student choir and a few teachers sing. All of the students had Santa hats on whilst swaying together to the carol.

As I walk past, someone taps my shoulder. "Amy, there you are. I'd like you to meet the school's governors. I've just been telling them about your audition for RADA." Mr Perkins looks rather smug as if he's showing me off.

I realised that this was the first time that someone more superior had talked about me to make themselves look good. It was a very unusual experience but one that I could grow fond of.

"It's a pleasure to meet you, Amy." One of the governors shakes my hand. but I can tell already that they're judging me. "Are you nervous at all about your audition?

"I am. Very much so, hopefully, with a lot of preparation, I might get a place." I'm already scratching my arm. I'm not sure how I'm going to get through the audition if I'm this nervous with something that's nowhere near as important as the audition.

The rest of the fair goes off without a hitch. After everyone has left, Josh and I stay to help clear up the glitter on the floor from the decorations and the several mulled wine glasses. After making sure that the hall is clean and tidy, I make my way to drama, which is just off the main hall, and given that my legs were aching, the close location is a blessing in disguise. I still haven't fully forgiven Miss Stevens for her behaviour in the first lesson we had together, although I need to put this behind me as I'm hoping that she will help me prepare for the audition.

Before I even open the door to the studio, I can hear everyone doing their vocal warm-up exercises, which, given my cerebral palsy, can be challenging.

"Amy, thank you for finally showing up!"

She never misses an opportunity to give me some attitude. I let this slide; it's not worth going down to her level.

We are working on our final showcases, which will then be performed in front of an audience at the end of February. I feel an enormous amount of pressure for this performance as I'm the first disabled student who has chosen drama as A-Level, and also everyone knows that I want to get into RADA. After Miss Stevens had set us our assignments is an excellent opportunity to ask her for some support.

"Can I help you, Miss Webb? You know what if you're

struggling with this subject, then maybe you shouldn't have chosen it?" She lowers her head and looks at me over her glasses; the nerves suddenly kick in.

I decide to ignore yet again one of her put-downs. "Miss Stevens, I don't know whether or not you have heard, but I've been invited for a RADA audition, so—"

"Yes, it looks like they will let anyone audition now. It certainly wasn't like that in my day!"

Even though her audition was only three years ago. I smile because, again, I'm trying to be the bigger person.

"So, with that in mind, I was wondering whether or not you could please help me prepare for my audition?"

She puts down the papers that she was obviously pretending to read whilst talking and looks straight at me. "I'm sorry, but given my expertise and experience, I can only give my support to those who actually have a shot of getting in!"

I'm gobsmacked, given that she probably has had some kind of action plan given by Mr Perkins after the last incident; I thought she would be a little more willing to make amends.

I take a deep breath and smile. "Well, Miss Stevens, I thought your job was to support and encourage each and every one of your students no matter what their abilities or disabilities? Although, given your attitude, I just want to say thank you."

"For what, Miss Webb?"

"For giving me the chance to now prove you wrong.

Given my past record, it's never a good idea to be in that position. See when anyone gives me even an inkling of doubt, it just drives me to fight for something even more." I turn my frame, walk over to the other side of the studio, and started to work on my Shakespeare monologue.

Finally, the end of the term has arrived. I'm exhausted and really looking forward to having some time off with the people who mean the most to me. If someone had told me a year ago that I would be appointed head girl in the first term of my final year, have an audition for one of the best drama schools in the country, and fallen in love with my best friend, I would not have believed them.

On the last day of term, I invite Josh and our deputy team over for a few festive treats and to watch a Christmas film. I clear this with Jack and his family before; they couldn't have been more supportive. Since Jack and I aren't organised enough to pick a film prior to everyone showing up, we decide to have a debate. After much deliberation, we agree that *Miracle on 34th Street* is the overall winner but the 1994 version and not the original black and white one. Jack and I curl up on one of their large chairs with many throw pillows surrounding us. One of the problems with having to walk with a frame is that it tends to end up in the way most of the time. Without making a fuss, Jack moves it to the other end of the room.

I would never have thought that at eighteen, I would have to decide about whose family we would see on Christmas Day. As a child, I always saw families arguing about who they would see on Christmas Day, which meant that the other side of the family would get the consolation prize of Boxing Day. I think it is only fair that I stay with Jack's family on Christmas Day. I don't want Mum to be on her own for Christmas, which is why I spoke to Amy a couple of days ago. She assured me that she would have Mum over to hers.

After all, they have made me feel so welcome living with them. The whole day is incredible. Jenny had personalised stockings for all of the family. As a surprise, she made me one as well. Jack's family is quite traditional with the whole day, roast turkey for lunch with all the trimmings, before retiring to the sofa to watch the Queen's Speech at 15:00. Jenny has always made sure that all her children have everything they wanted and more on any typical day. She definitely went the extra mile with it being Christmas. Having moved in just a few weeks ago, I am fully prepared to take a back seat. Jack makes sure that I am always included and feel special.

After the Queen's Speech, we sit around the Christmas tree and exchange gifts. I've never seen so many gifts around one tree; however, given that there was so many of them, it makes sense that they were spreading along the front room. Jenny puts on some Christmas music in the background just in case it doesn't feel festive enough. She then sits down on the floor beside the tree while the rest of us are spread out across the room. "Ok, as our guest, I think Amy should get the first present."

I'm surprised by this; she hands me a beautiful wrap box-shaped present with silver and white snowflake wrapping paper.

I say, "Oh, thank you so much for this, but you really didn't have to."

Mark pats me on the back. "Welcome to the family, not that you weren't beforehand."

I slowly undo the ribbon and then tore open the wrapping paper. Inside was the complete collection of Scrubs box set.

They've obviously seen me watching it in Jack's room. "Oh, thank you so much! I don't know what to say."

Jack smiles. "We've finally done it! She's speechless! I was beginning to believe this moment would never come!"

I kiss him and then hold onto my frame, get up from the sofa and walk over to hug both Jenny and Mark.

As I sit back down, Jack says, "Does this mean that I'm not going to see you for the rest of the week?" He crosses his fingers.

"You wish!" I playfully push him on the arm.

The rest of the family digs into their presents. Marcus, Ben, and Harry all have big boxes of toys and craft supplies that they want to get stuck into straight away. As Mia and

Beth are a little bit older than the boys, Jenny and Mark bought them a Netflix subscription and a few vouchers so that they can choose what they want when they go shopping in the January sales. I always find it amazing growing up that as I get older, somehow the presents got smaller but cost more.

After all the presents have been opened, Jack's youngest nephew Harry starts a wrapping paper fight. Jack has always told me that it's a tradition within their household. After a while, wrapping paper covers the whole of the living room floor. Jenny comes back in from the kitchen with a giant bin bag and began clearing up the wrapping paper scattered all over the floor. I hold onto my frame and start to pick the pieces up as it is unfair for her to do it all by herself.

"Oh! You didn't have to do that, dear. I'm used to it, living in this household," she says as she stands up to brush the hair off her face.

"It's my pleasure. You've done so much for me over the last few weeks; it's the least I could do." I put pieces of wrapping paper into the bag.

"Well, you certainly make my son happy, that's for sure, not that you didn't before, but I have seen a change in him recently. He's so much calmer and really focusing on his future." Jenny has always been so welcoming; since we've been dating, she hasn't commented much on anything that has been going on between Jack and me, so I've been unsure whether she is happy about her son dating me or not.

"Really? You think so?"

She smiles. "Amy, there's no one else who is more perfectly matched for him than you. You two just fit perfectly together."

Jack walks back into the living room with a glass of champagne for him and a glass of non-alcoholic wine whilst kissing me on the forehead. "What's going on?"

He hands me my drink and puts his arm around my waist.

"Oh nothing, son, just girl talk," she says as she winks at me. Jenny knows he won't ask any more questions; it's sort of a girl code. She carries on putting the wrapping in the bag and then walks out the back door to assumably put it in the bin.

As I look around the room, I realise that even though this wasn't my original plan of how I wanted to spend Christmas, I couldn't be happier. Seeing the kids surrounded by their presents and the look of pure joy on their faces showed me what Christmas is actually about.

Just as quickly as it arrives, Christmas is already over. However, with New Year's just around the corner, it's a chance for new beginnings and fresh starts. As I sit on my bed whilst getting dressed, I reflect on this year. It has been full of drama, a lot of it I wasn't expecting. I have had to use every ounce of courage and determination that I've got in me to keep going. I've shown myself how strong I am even in the toughest of times. There have been some fantastic highlights; somehow, I became head girl. I'm still unsure how that happened. I've fallen in love with my best friend and couldn't be happier with his ongoing support and endless love. I'm also so thankful for Emma and Josie for keeping me grounded and making me see how I should be treated. I can't wait to see them on New Year's Eve to hopefully see in what I hope to be an unforgettable year.

I'm running a highlights reel in my head, just like the one from the last episode of *Scrubs.* After spending a moment or two in my own little world, I realise that Jack is watching me and smiling. "What?"

"Nothing, babe, I just don't think I could be any happier than I am right now. Also, I could tell that you were deep in thought because you were doing that weird thing with your lips." He kisses me softly and then wraps his arms around me.

"Me neither, baby; I love you so much. What weird thing with my lips?"

"Really? I thought you knew. Basically, it's like you're mumbling to yourself, but don't worry, it's cute."

Great, one more thing to add to the list of things that make me self-conscious, not that it wasn't long enough already.

It is the day before New Year's Eve which is the only way I remember what day it is at the moment. For some reason, the week between Christmas and New Year, nobody knows the actual day. I always find it hilarious how some TV shows do their "Christmas Special" when all it is is just a bit of tinsel in the studio or a big tree, and then suddenly it's a Christmas show. However, when you've got a large tub of Roses or Celebrations on your lap, anything is interesting. Jack and I definitely balance each other as he doesn't like the strawberry dreams in the tin, whereas they are my favourite. I can't really eat the toffee's as I struggle to chew them and usually choke on them; thankfully, they're Jack's favourite. That evening both Jack and I end up falling asleep on the sofa snuggled under a blanket.

I'm awoken the next morning to the sound of a vacuum cleaner; I'm not quite sure how I made it upstairs last night. Jenny must be getting ready for the party. There aren't many problems with living at Jack's; however, I have to wait for Jack to wake up before I can go downstairs. I shouldn't really complain as his parents are letting me stay here rent-free. As Jack gets to the bottom step whilst I'm in his arms, I notice all the fantastic decorations covering their front room. Several banners say "happy new year" or "2017." Jack comes back down again with my frame.

"Thank you, baby"

"Anything for you. By the way, you look incredible in my hoodie." His cheeky smile never fails to make me feel like the luckiest girl in the world.

"I know, and by the way, you're not getting this back."

His hoodies are so cosy, and the smell of Hugo Boss is irresistible.

As I walk through to the kitchen, Jenny's preparing several platters of cocktail sausages, sausage rolls, chicken skewers and several bowls of crisps for guests to nibble on. "Is there anything I can help you with, Jenny?"

She looks up at me and smiles. "Oh, thanks, dear, but not really; it's sort of done; oh, there are some balloons that need pumping up." She goes into a bag on the dining table and gives us a bag of balloons and a pump.

As I struggle with tying the balloons, Jack and I develop a system where I pump them up and then pass them to him to tie. After about half an hour, the entire carpet is covered in balloons.

Jack suddenly looks up at me and smiles. "I can't imagine seeing the new year in with anyone else."

As his lips press against mine, we are unfortunately by Mark; I still find it a bit awkward kissing Jack in front of his parents. "Oh, sorry, you two! Young love, I definitely do miss it."

Jenny comes out from the kitchen. "What do you mean you miss it? Are you saying that we are now just old and now stuck with each other?"

He quickly rushes to the kitchen, keeping his head down, probably so he doesn't get into any more trouble than he already is in.

A few moments pass as I am pumping up another balloon, and Mark pops his head around the corner into the living room where we are sitting. "Oh, Amy, I remembered to get the wine that you can drink so that there is something for you to toast at midnight."

I love Jack's family; they always remember the small details so that I never feel left out or awkward.

A little later, Jack and I are getting ready. I spoilt myself and bought a new dress with some of the money that Mum had given me for Christmas. It is covered with multi-coloured sequins, perfect for the occasion. I pair it with black boots and put black tinsel around my frame. I curl my hair and do my classic go-to smoky eye and a nude lip. Jack comes into the guest room. Even though his family want me to call it my room, I don't feel comfortable enough yet.

"Wow! I must be the lucky one tonight! You look absolutely stunning." He comes behind me as I am finishing my make-up; he wraps his arms around my stomach, making my heart skip a beat.

"Well, mister, you started the year as a real player. Who would have thought you'd now be in a serious relationship?"

He turns me around and kisses me. "Amy, I wanted to say this at midnight."

My heart fills with excitement and anticipation.

Jack is rubbing his hands together; he is red in the face, and I can tell he is nervous. "Amy, I've been building up to say this for a while now; I love you! You're amazing, and I find it so attractive how driven you are to make the world a better place."

Never did I think that these words would've come out of his mouth first. We've said it jokingly before like teenagers do. I can tell that this time was different; this time, he means it.

He adds, "I don't want you to feel that you have to say it as—"

"I love you too."

Instantly, I can physically see a weight being lifted of Jack's shoulders. He picks me up and kisses me in a way that he has never done before; it is like we now have an even deeper connection.

Jack's family knows how to throw a party; fantastic music, great food and all his family are so welcoming. Even though I've known Jack since we were young, I've never really met any of his family apart from his parents, siblings, nieces, and nephews. Luckily, Jack's house is much larger than ours. There's no way we could have this many people at ours unless we stood like sardines! I realise that this was the first party that Jack and I have attended as an official couple. Jenny is determined to let everyone and anyone know this.

The time has come that everyone waits for on New Years' Eve, the countdown! Jenny had turned the TV on to watch the fireworks that they do on the London Eye. I always wonder how cold the people are that are standing right at the front. There is only a minute to go when Jack sits down next to me with a glass of wine.

He puts his arm around me. "This is it, a new start with the love of my life."

Just then, everyone in the room shouts, "3,2,1 HAPPY NEW YEAR!" The fireworks have started.

I say to Jack, "Happy new year, baby. I love you."

Our lips interlock, and I don't care if anybody is watching. "I think this is going to be our best year yet."

It instantly feels like it is just him and me in the entire world. It is like in one of those movies when everybody else is blurred out. Your only focus is on the two main characters sharing this incredible, passionate kiss, and for some reason, it's always raining within these scenes. Starting the year with someone who truly loves me, that's new.

We are only knocked back to reality when Jenny comes over and sloppily kisses us both on the cheek. "I love you guys both so much." Her words are slurred due to having one too many red wines, but who cares? It's New Year's, after all.

chapter 11

Everything has ramped up a gear since returning to school from the Christmas break. There are only four months to go until my exams, and I am nowhere near ready. As usual, I have several meetings with Mr Perkins and the student council which has been interesting. Within these meetings, you soon learn who is being a representative for ego and who actually cares about the school.

Since being appointed head girl, there have been mixed reviews. Most of the year group and, in fact, the school are delighted for me and feel that I deserved it for sure. As always with everything I do, they are a small group of idiots that feel and have vocalised that I only got it due to teachers feeling sorry for me. I actually appreciate these people as I know these opinions are most likely shared because they are jealous. It can't help but get to me though just a little bit;

after all, I'm only human.

I'm so glad that Jack and I spent all of the two weeks we had off together as I've hardly seen him since we have been back. I've either been completing coursework for the relevant subjects, fulfilling my duties as head girl, trying my best to meet all my deadlines, or getting as much preparation as possible in, before my audition.

I wake up the following morning feeling like my stomach was about to explode. I could throw up at any moment. The day that everything comes down to has finally arrived. Over the weekend, I ensured that I have everything prepared over the weekend: train tickets booked, knowing which tubes we had to get to the school. I have my black t-shirt and leggings ironed folded nicely in my bag as I don't want to get them dirty on the train. My reading material is all organised in a smart black portfolio, even though I have already memorised everything I need for the audition. I'm almost reciting it in my sleep.

Jack isn't impressed about getting a train at twenty pasts seven in the morning. My audition isn't until ten, but I want to make sure that we have plenty of time. He managed to get the day off; I'm not quite sure how, but I've learnt with Jack the less I know the better. I made sure that the seats on the train have enough room for my frame to fit as well. These are things that you, unfortunately, have to think of when you have cerebral palsy. I also had to make sure that I had all the appropriate medication in case we were home late. These things are a must for me as if I don't feel like I'm organised, I become anxious, which isn't an option right now. I was in two minds about the audition on one hand, I'm amazed that I even got an invitation. Although, as always, I have doubt in the back of my mind that I will automatically be ruled out just because I use a walking frame. Although, I have to constantly remind myself that they can't do this as it would be discrimination.

Jack and I make our way to the platform as we have priority access seats, so I don't have to worry about getting pushed. I booked a table seat for the both of us so that we could have breakfast that Jack had picked up on the way to the station. I can also use the time to make sure that I know all of my reading material.

Eventually, I settle into the journey and enjoy looking at the scenery to try and calm my nerves. I can see in the reflection two elderly ladies are coming on the train and sitting at the table next to us. Jack sits opposite me as he wants to make sure that I'm facing forward.

He holds my hand and strokes my thumb as he can tell how nervous I am. "It's going to be alright; you've done so much prep I almost know the script off by heart. I know you're going to smash it."

I smiled; I'm so grateful to have such a supportive boyfriend by my side; he has made this process that little bit easier.

One of the two elderly ladies smiles once again at us; she

then looks at Jack. "It must be such a fulfilling role. I bet your parents are proud."

Jack and I look at each other, confused.

"I'm sorry? What do you mean by that?" I ask.

The elderly lady looks confused by my reply. Jack and I don't break our stares.

"Oh, my apologies, dear, isn't he your brother?"

What? How many siblings does she know that hold hands?

Jack kisses me and then looks right back at her. I'm unsure if she is gobsmacked or confused, but she doesn't say a word to us for the rest of the journey. Once we arrive in London, we need to get on the Hammersmith & City line to get over to RADA. Jack gets my frame down from the luggage storage above us and goes in front of me so that no one can push in whilst I am getting off the train.

"I can't believe that! Who does she think she is? Am I your carer? Yeah, just because you used a walking frame and have a disability means you can't have a boyfriend. Some people are so narrow-minded!" Jack says.

I sometimes forget that Jack isn't used to dealing with this kind of judgement. "Babe, calm down!"

He gets redder in the face.

I say, "I know it's wrong to think that just because I use a walking frame means that I can't be in a relationship. That's just how it is, so please just let it go. We can't change someone's opinions straight away. Believe me, I've tried. What we can do is control how we react to this discriminative behaviour, ok? Jack, I've had to put up with this sort of discrimination my whole life. People are always going to judge me on something; usually, it's because they don't understand what's it's like to have a disability."

Jack getting wound up isn't going to help anyone, but I completely understand his frustration. I've never understood it either, no matter how many times I've tried. In theory, this judgement is saying that we should only date people who are exactly like us. How boring would that be? Also, it's extremely discriminative.

Finally, it's real; no turning back now. We need to get the lift out of the tube station and walk the short distance from the station to the school. I stop outside the main gates, awed that I'm finally here. All I can think of is being six and announcing to Mum whilst we were on holiday that I wanted to be on the West End when I was older. Now is my chance to hopefully start the journey of making those dreams come true.

The actual building sticks out to me like a bright spotlight shining down from the sky. The entrance is grand, with large glass panels covering the front of the building and their iconic flag on the side flapping in the wind.

Jack walks in front of me. "This is it! Good luck, I love you. I'm so proud of you."

He kisses my cheek and I say, "Oh wait, what are you going to do?"

He laughs and says, "Don't worry about me. This is your day. Just text me when you're done. Love you so much, I'm so proud of you."

He strides up the street. I take a deep breath and walk through the door. As I've had a walking frame since I was two, I have developed a knack for opening doors independently by using the frame as a doorstop so that I can get through. As I walk through the airy, bright foyer, I notice a lady on reception who was holding a clipboard.

"May I help you?" She smiles at me; unfortunately, I can tell straight away that she is judging me based on the walking frame.

"Um, yes, good morning. I'm here for an audition?

"Name?" She looks down at her clipboard.

"Amy Webb."

She moves her pen down the clipboard. "Ah yes, there you are. If you would like to take a seat." She checks her watch. "The audition doesn't start for another half an hour, so if you want to get a cup of coffee or tea, then please help yourself."

I head to a bunch of comfy sofas and chairs on the right-hand side of the large entrance hall. The building seems both historical and modern at the same time, with large windows letting in the winter sun, while still having large stone pillars throughout the space. Without even looking, I can feel that several of the people already are staring.

"Hi, I'm Amy." I always find that if I introduce myself, people feel awkward for not responding, so they are almost forced to make a conversation if only for a minute. Throughout the next half an hour, several other candidates arrive and come to sit down. At this point, I decide to go and get into my black outfit to prepare for the audition.

The lady comes over a little while later and asks us to all go through to the drama studio. I pick up my backpack, throw it over my shoulder and start walking with the rest of the auditionees. Thankfully, one of them kindly holds the heavy door open for me. I head into the studio. Bright theatre lights illuminate the stage. On my right is a table in the middle of the audience. Three people sit behind it.

The middle woman stands up. "Welcome, candidates, to RADA. Congratulations for getting this far. If you could all take a seat on the top row, we will then proceed."

The seats are on tiers, meaning that there's a step to every row. I either have to ask for some assistance or sit on the front row, making me look eager. I decide to go for the second option as I don't want to draw attention to myself even though I know it will probably look a bit weird.

Thankfully, I'm right where I want in the line-up of auditions, in the middle. This means that I still have time to prepare myself emotionally and physically but won't be waiting around for ages. While waiting, we're escorted to another room where I start chatting to some of the other candidates and having the usual conversations with someone you've just met about where we've grown up or what made us apply. I am a little apprehensive about revealing too much about myself because of the sperm donor.

With only thirty places available and fifty of us; the competition is intense. I know the odds aren't great, but at this point, I've got as much of a chance as anyone else.

One of the runners helping with the auditions, who is a current RADA student, calls, "Amy Webb?"

This is it! Two years of preparation and a childhood dream has now come down to the next ten minutes.

I follow the runner into the audition room; the panel all greets me with a smile, which feels reassuring. "Is it Amy?"

I clear my throat ."Yes. It is."

I'm shaking with nerves.

Thankfully, she smiles back at me. "So, what made you apply to RADA?"

I'm so glad she asked this question because it's one of the ones that I've prepped for.

"Well, it's always been a dream of mine to appear on the West End as an actress. It's also my mission to make the sector more inclusive."

She smiles and nods her head as if she agrees with me. Beads of sweat start to trickle down my face due to the hot stage lights and the pressure of the audition.

"I couldn't agree with you more, and I certainly couldn't have said it better myself. Well, Amy, whenever you're ready, just remember to relax and pretend like we are not even here."

She knows I'm nervous. I take a minute to calm myself and used some breathing techniques that I've learnt. I then let go of my frame with one hand so that I can project with my body as well as my voice. I start to perform my memorised monologue and make sure that I use the correct tone and pitch for Juliet to make it more believable and realistic instead of just memorising text. I make sure that I'm thinking about playing my age because I know that's what they will be looking for.

I'm about halfway through my monologue when I get interrupted. "Hi Amy, I'm Nicole, one of the vocal coaches here. What you're saying is good; unfortunately, we can't actually hear you. Can you just remember to project your voice and make sure that you're constantly thinking about making your character believable!"

Having done research prior, I know that this was quite normal. Usually, they want to give you direction to make your audition even better. I'm a little stunned about this. Usually projecting my voice is the least of my concerns. I smile and prepare myself to give it another shot. I start to perform my monologue again when suddenly I just freeze.

"Ok, well, thank you for that."

Unfortunately, as I've seen so many audition videos generally when they thank you for coming in, it means you're done.

I have to do something. "No, no, I'm sorry, but can I have one more chance, please?"

Nicole folds her arms. "Why?"

I'm startled by this comment.

"Because I've been dreaming about this since I was little, becoming an actress on the West End is all I've ever wanted to do. I don't want to throw away my chance just like that!"

Thankfully, she gestures for me to have one more try.

I take a deep breath, have a quick plea with the universe for everything to be on my side just for the next few minutes. After all, given the cards that it already dealt me, it certainly owes me. Luckily it works; I get through the whole monologue without any hiccups. I can feel my entire body relax with an overwhelming sense of relief.

As I compose myself, planning for the worst and hoping for the best, I notice that Edward Kemp, the actual director of RADA, who wrote to me, is in the wings watching my performance. I am so relieved that I didn't see him prior to this; it definitely would've set my nerves over the edge.

He walks onto the stage whilst smiling. "Amy, it's a pleasure to meet you finally. I'm glad that I got to see your performance or at least the end. I really do admire you for what you're trying to achieve. I love what you wrote in your email regarding this audition. You're absolutely right about individuals with disabilities don't always get the chance to follow their dreams due to discrimination or people being too ignorant to understand."

"It's a pleasure to meet you, Edward. Thank you! I believe that everyone should have the chance to be whoever they want to be. Society doesn't always accept people disabilities because we are too different from others. I would rather someone ask me about what disabilities I've got than assume or just ignore me. I believe that we all have a disability in one way or another because nobody is perfect." This is my one chance to show who I was and why I do what I do. I can't afford to mess this up.

Nicole has made her way up to the stage along with the other judges to greet Edward.

He smiles back at me. "Well, thank you for taking the time to audition for us; we will be in touch soon."

I smile back at all of them and take my cue to find the exit. I can hear them muttering behind me, but it isn't right to stop and try and work out what they are saying.

Due to it being rush hour, the train is absolutely packed. It's hot, sticky and has an overwhelming scent of urine. I can't reserve seats for the train home. Fortunately, a kind gentleman who was reading the Metro Newspaper gives his seat up to me whilst Jack stands over me to keep me safe.

He kisses my forehead. "I'm still really proud of you. You have to keep telling yourself that you did the best you could."

Since I came out of the audition an hour ago in floods of tears, he has been amazing. After two hours of travelling, we are finally home. I am exhausted and struggle to put one foot in front of the other. Jack orders a pizza on the way home so that neither of us would have to cook. He gets the timing of ordering perfect. Just as we walk through the door, there is a knock. As my legs are hurting so much, Jack suggests eating it on his bed whilst watching Netflix.

I wake up the following day, and my head was pounding. All I want to do is watch Netflix and eat chocolate all day. I reluctantly drag myself out of bed with just enough time to get ready for school. My muscles are aching so much that I need help from Jenny getting dressed. I hate when this happens especially when you've got to ask your boyfriend's parents.

Throughout the whole of my morning lessons, I feel lightheaded. Every time I stand up, I feel like I am about to collapse. Jack is highly concerned and makes sure that I get into each classroom instead of just saying goodbye at the door. Thankfully, I am allowed to have food during lessons. I always had an emergency Freddo in my bag if these situations should occur. I'm glad when lunchtime finally comes around, as usually in these situations eating a meal boosts my energy levels back to normal. Going home isn't an option as I don't want Jack to feel like he needs to leave school. I think about texting Mum, but she's been through enough already; I'll be fine.

As I'm making my way down to the canteen, the world spins around me. My arms tingle. I have pins and needles everywhere, causing me so much pain. Without any warning, I collapse to the floor. I can't focus on what was going on around me as everything spins around me. I can feel my body uncontrollably twitching. I grow hotter and hotter by the second. Tears stream down my face. I am in unbearable pain. I can sense someone stroking my hair but can't focus on who it was.

Suddenly, I can hear a recognisable voice. "No, don't move her. She's having an epileptic seizure. We need to time it; then, when she has stopped, we can move her into the recovery position."

I can sense that I am crying unable to stop myself. Then, I feel someone hold my hand. "Baby, it's me. Everything is going to be ok. You're having a fit. Try and relax. I'm not going to leave you."

Jack's hand is stroking my face; immediately, I felt a sense of relief. I am safe.

"Right, everyone needs to move back, and someone needs to call an ambulance. This is the first fit she has had in years." Jack's still holding my hand.

My body aches so much because of the spasms, and I can't control them. Dribble trickles down, and my mouth becomes dryer and dryer by the second.

Then there's a teacher's voice. I am unsure who it was, but they say, "Um, Jack, maybe you should go to the main hall to get some lunch. We've got this."

Jack strokes his thumb against mine. "No, she needs to

know I'm here. After all, I'm her boyfriend, and I want to know that she's ok. So, I'll be going to the hospital with her as well, ok!"

Hearing a voice that I don't recognise panics me. "Ok Amy, my name is Rob, and I'm one of the paramedics."

He talks to Jack. Suddenly, a blood pressure cuff tightens around my arm and an oxygen mask covers my mouth. One of them asks Jack about my medical history.

"I'm her boyfriend, but I have known Amy since we were young."

The paramedic asks Jack some questions. Next thing I know, they stick a thermometer in my ear then I can feel Rob's arm on my shoulder, and Jack still holding my other hand. "What time did the seizure start?"

Jack let go of my hand. "It was about five past twelve."

Rob says, "Ok, that means that she had been in it for twenty minutes and is still unresponsive".

"Is that bad?" Jack sounded even more worried.

"I'm recommending that we get her to the hospital and seen by a doctor. Right, can we create some space please as we need to get the stretcher through. Amy? Can you hear me? What we're going to do is pop you up to the hospital and have you seen by a doctor. Don't worry, everything's going to be alright."

I am aware of my surroundings at this point and am trying to focus on Rob.

"Hello, Amy, how are you feeling? Ok, I make that 12:25

for getting a response from the patient. It seems as though she's starting to come around."

My body has relaxed a little bit but was still in a lot of pain. I could then feel them pick me up and put me on what felt like a bed. My hand is still twitching as I am wheeled out of the school doors and then onto the ambulance. My whole right side of my body completely aches, and it is an effort even to turn my head.

Being wheeled onto the ambulance feels like someone has punched me in the stomach. I can see Jack following behind me with my bag and coat. He smiles at me but still looks very concerned. Rob opens up one of the seats in the back of the ambulance for him to sit on. The entire journey to hospital I keep focused on Jack. He keeps mouthing that he loves me and strokes my thumb.

chapter 12

My head pounds. My neck is stiff, and my lips are parched. It takes me a few minutes to figure out where I am. As I try to move my arms to stretch, I notice an IV cannula in one hand. The other has a heart rate monitor on my index finger; it doesn't take a genius to work out what has happened. I have two of those hospital bracelets, one on each wrist with my name and date of birth on. As I look over to the whiteboard, which is on the wall next to my bed, I noticed several times written on it; I work out that this means I've had more fits. It instantly fills me with fear. As I try to move and to stretch, my whole body is in unbearable pain.

Jack stands up from the chair situated next to my bed. "Hey beautiful, how are you feeling?". It takes me a few minutes to focus on him as my brain is still trying to process what is going on. He kisses me on the forehead, which feels reassuring.

He holds onto my hand and strokes my thumb again as I ask, “What happened? Why am I here?”

A doctor appears from behind the curtain and stands next to my bed. “Hello Amy. My name is Dr Strong. I’m one of the neurology consultants here.”

I’m confused as to why a neurology consultant is by the side of my bed.

He says, “You’ve had several seizures; therefore, we need to monitor you over the next few hours as to why this has happened”.

Jack looks concerned. “Babe, I don’t want you to worry.”

I automatically worry.

“You had a seizure at school;. Just relax you’re in good hands. I promise I won’t leave your side.” He kisses me on the hand that doesn’t have the giant needle in it.

“I what? But how?” Dizzy, I struggle to focus on anything. As I try to sit up, my body just slumps back down as though it had turned into jelly. It’s like my brain and body are disconnected. Everything I tell my body to do isn’t working.

Jack continues, “Well, I got told by one of my mates who saw it happen that you were walking to lunch when you just collapsed.”

Every muscle is tensing up. I’m unable to relax. “Hang on; you weren’t there?”

I can tell instantly Jack felt terrible.

"I was on my way to meet you when I saw a large group of people surrounding someone. When I realised it was you in the middle of it, I immediately pushed everyone out the way to get to you. Luckily, a few teachers moved everyone on before you started twitching," he says.

I'm a little bit relieved that the whole of the school didn't see me go properly into one as I know watching a seizure can be quite scary. "So, hang on, how come you stayed? Oh no, Jack, are you going to get into trouble for bunking off school again?"

He looks directly at me. "Well, I love you. I wanted to make sure that you weren't going to go through this alone and not just for this fit, always. Don't worry. Mr Perkins said I could go."

Dr Strong has been writing on a clipboard all this time. "Amy, what I suggest we do is observe you for the next few hours, and if you seem well enough to recover at home, we will discharge you today. My main concern at the moment is we don't know what set off your seizure."

Suddenly, Mum is round the other side of my bed to Jack asking what's happened. Jack suggests that they discuss this outside because he doesn't want me to hear the story all over again.

He kisses me. "I'll be back in a minute, love you." Jack has his arm around Mum as they walk out of the ward.

As I look around me, all I can see are machines and hospital carts filled with medicines and equipment. The side curtain to my bay is closed across, but the front one is wide open so that the doctors and nurses can keep an eye on me. There are several screams of pain from the bay next to me. There's no way I am going to sleep in here. My head starts to feel dizzy again.

Dr Strong says, "She's going into one again."

Suddenly, there's a whole team of doctors and nurses around me. I can hear a trolley coming into the bay.

One of them put an oxygen mask over me. "Amy, we're just going to put this on to help you breathe."

Jack says, "What happened? Baby?"

One of the nurses explains to him that I am going into another seizure. I can feel Jack stroking my face as he says, "I'm here, baby, just relax. It's going to be ok."

Mum is talking to one of the nurses, but I can't work out what they're saying. After a few minutes, my body stops. I immediately fall asleep.

Whilst Jack is still holding my hand, he says, "Jo, I haven't really seen Amy have many fits. What do I do?"

I think he is unaware that I can actually hear him as I am drifting in and out of sleep.

"Oh, my lovely, there's nothing we can do. I just hope that we can get her out of here soon as she will recover so much quicker at home. Hopefully, as long as she doesn't have any more seizures, Dr Strong should discharge her."

I wake several hours later and notice that I am no longer

in the curtained bay; I have been moved onto a ward and I can see it's night. This doesn't help my mood in the slightest as I take this to mean I am now staying in overnight, my worst nightmare. Thankfully, Mum and Jack are still by my bedside, which is the only bit of comfort in this strange situation. Jack sits on the end of my bed, watching every single detail, which creeps me out a bit, but I know he's only doing it because he's so worried. Mum is sitting on one of those tall-backed chairs by the side of my bed.

Suddenly my phone starts ringing inside my bag. Mum pulls my bag onto the bed, and I reach into the pocket and pull the phone out; it's a blocked number. Jack takes the phone out of my hand. I ama little offended by this; however, given the amount of medication I currently have in my body, maybe it's for the best. "Hello, no, this is her boyfriend. Unfortunately, Amy's actually in hospital at the moment." He pauses. "Ok, I'll tell her, thanks bye".

I look at him very apprehensively. "Who was it?"

His tone of voice completely changes. "Um, babe, I don't think this is the best time to discuss it, but they will give you a call in a couple of days."

"Jack?" He is looking everywhere else but, in my direction, which makes me even more anxious as I demand, "WHO WAS IT?"

I know it is something bad; otherwise, he would've told me straight away to make me feel better.

"Ams, the only thing you need to worry about right now

is getting better." He kisses my forehead and holds tightly onto my hand, locking each of his fingers into mine.

Even though I desperately wanted to know what the phone call was about, I know Jack is right. I start to shiver as my body becomes unbearably cold. Jack immediately takes off his hoodie and wraps it around my shoulders. There's something about wearing his hoodie that instantly makes me feel better.

After a few hours, Dr Strong comes back to see me. "Hello Amy, how are you feeling?"

"I feel extremely tired and drained." My speech is still slightly slurred; he immediately nodded like he was expecting this response.

"Well, Amy, given how many seizures you have had and that this hasn't happened for many years, I think that it's best if we keep you in overnight for observation. We will need you to have an CT in the morning and we hope to send you home tomorrow if no more seizures occur overnight."

I suspected this would be the case but had hoped for a better outcome. The wards are very similar to paediatrics which I've been in countless times before. However, there are fewer giraffes on the walls, and the nurses aren't wearing brightly coloured scrubs with clowns or butterflies covering them. There is no playroom/school on the ward, which there was when I was little. It was the only good thing about being in hospital back then.

Soon after Dr Strong leaves, a nurse comes around to ask

what I want for breakfast and offers me a sandwich now as I'd missed dinner. Given that this isn't my first time in hospital, I know that the food isn't always the best.

Jack pipes up "Babe, why don't I go and get you a panini from downstairs? Can I get you anything, Jo?"

That's one of the many reasons why I love him. He doesn't just love me but also treats Mum as a third parent.

"Oh Jack, thanks, sweetheart. I'd love a cup of coffee, please? Let me give you some money." Mum rattles around in her purse. "I'm so used to having to sort myself out when we're in the hospital."

"Jo, don't worry about it. This one is on me." Jack kisses my forehead before going to get my favourite ham and cheese panini from the Costa coffee shop downstairs. I don't, however, turn down the jelly and ice cream that the nurse had found for me.

Just as I was about to drift off on a downwards spiral of feeling that I'm not good enough for Jack, there is my knight in shining armour!

"What's up? I can see that's something is bothering you." He interlocks his fingers inside of mine.

"It's nothing. Don't worry about it." I turn away to hide the tears.

"Amy, you know I can read you like a book. Now, come on what's up?"

"I'm just worried about you."

Jack looks at me confused. Mum is trying to hide in the

corner, but I can tell that this is awkward for her.

"Look, I know this hasn't been easy for to deal with and I'm just aware that I could have another seizure just as bad or even worse. So, if you want to go to being just friends then I completely understand," I say.

Immediately, Jack just burst out with laughter.

"Jack, I'm serious!"

"I know and that's why I love you. Amy, you really think I'm going to stop loving you just because you've had a seizure?" He looks at me like he can't believe what I'm saying. "Amy, I've known you long enough to know what problems you come with, and I still won't change you for the world. You're one of the strongest people I know and if you think I am running out on you then maybe you need another brain scan because obviously there's been more damage than we thought." He starts to chuckle.

Another hour passes, and a nurse comes around with medication for each of the patients on the ward.

I suddenly panic. "Mum, Mum! We didn't bring my medication! Oh, no, what if I have another fit again?"

Mum starts to stroke my arm to try and console me. "Darling, shh, don't worry. We're in a hospital. They have rooms and rooms full of tablets and anyway, your medication is likely to change so that you can control your seizures again." She seems very relaxed about the situation.

The nurse hands me a small plastic cup with my normal three tablets inside it, plus an extra orange one.

"I'm sorry, but this isn't mine," I say, picking out the unknown tablet.

The nurse smiles at me. "Dr Strong is aware of this; however, he wants you to try this medication in the hope that it will control your seizures."

I throw the four tablets down my throat and gulp some water. I think the new tablet is meant to make me feel drowsy because a short while after that, I am incredibly sleepy. At this point, Mum and Jack had to say their goodbyes. That's another thing with adult wards; they don't like anyone staying with the patient overnight. I am so used to being in paediatrics where Mum could stay with me. I heave a sudden panic because I haven't seen my frame in hours. Thankfully, I needn't have worried as it is all folded up next to the cupboard by my bed.

Given that I haven't had a fit in such a long time, I'd forgotten how it doesn't just mess up your head but, in fact, your whole body. Even the simplest of tasks, such as brushing my teeth before going to sleep, can feel like a marathon. Mum must have brought me in an overnight bag as she had sorted lots of things out including putting my phone on charge and making sure I had my own pyjamas; wearing your own clothes in hospital can help aid recovery; having these home comforts makes me feel like I've got some control when the rest of my body is messed up.

Sleeping in a hospital isn't exactly easy due to all the beeping machinery. Also, patients can arrive on the wards from

A&E throughout the night, this isn't exactly helpful when you've got a neurological condition making sleep essential for your brain to restart. After a few hours of going in and out of sleep, I decide to give up.

The one thing that makes me relax when all else fails is music. I put on my instrumental playlist, which always sends me to sleep. As I pick up my phone, there are several messages waiting for me.

Jack texted, *"I'll be there at eight tomorrow; fingers crossed we can get you home. Love you lots, baby xx, and the whole family sends you their love, we all miss you xx."*

And there was another one from Josie. *"Hey hun, I've just heard what happened at school, here if you need anything. Love you, girl xx."*

I can tell even through a text that she is worried about me.

As I scroll through social media, there are so many messages on my wall from people I hardly speak to saying, "get well soon" or "sorry to hear about what happened at school, message me if you need anything." I'm surprised that I have so many messages, but I suppose that's what happens when you're head girl and have a seizure at school; word sort of gets around.

I must have drifted off to sleep at some point as I wake up to the sun shining through the window. The curtains are still drawn to the other side of my bed, but I can hear voices and what sounds like equipment moving around the ward.

A team of doctors and nurses start walking around each bed to get an update on each patient. This is also really new to me because they usually would talk to Mum while I would be doing some colouring or watching a movie. This time I am on my own, and I have to tell them how I feel. It's a very nerving experience when you're surrounded by a whole team of doctors and nurses making notes on every single little detail.

Dr Strong leads the group. "Good morning, Amy. How are you feeling?"

Now I know how animals feel at the zoo, I suddenly have ten people staring at me, commenting on every detail without any warning. I know, however, that I have to be honest with them even if that means staying in hospital even longer.

"A lot better, thanks. I'm still exhausted. I just hope that I can go home today?"

The whole team smiles at me. I don't want to tell them the whole truth. The fact that I'm scared that it may happen again. What if I'm on my own? Then my mind goes to a dark place. What if I have a seizure and I don't wake up? What if my disabilities get worse and I am no longer the person I've worked so hard to be? Quickly, I snap out of this. I know negative thinking never helps me.

"Well, we feel it's best if you continue to recover at home. Over the next few weeks, you'll need to take it easy and following the new medication plan that we've given you," the doctor says.

I am about to say that that was going to be quite hard to do given all the commitments I have; luckily, I don't.

"We feel that you may have outgrown the dose that you're currently on, which may also be the cause of your seizures. You might, over the next few days, experience something called Todd's paresis, which is just weakness in the legs caused by your body twitching during the seizure. I've seen from your notes that you're currently on a physio plan to strengthen your core. I recommend you taking it easy for the next couple of weeks and maybe only do one exercise a day. The pharmacist will be round shortly to explain to you the new doses and when you need to take them. You'll also be taken for your CT scan this morning. However, this is goodbye from me. I will be sending you a letter in the next few days for a date for a check-up in the next few months."

I'm not surprised about this decision, given that I have been on this dosage since I was eleven, so now being eighteen, I think it's time for a review.

I send a group text to Jack and Mum as I know that the one I don't text first will be offended. "*Doctors say I can go home today! Yay! However, I just need to get my brain scanned wait for them to change my meds xxx.*"

Within seconds I receive a message back from Jack like he has been waiting for this.

"Yes! Baby girl! Such a relief. lots of Netflix and chill days for you then (and I actually mean Netflix and chill). Love you and am so glad to hear that you're ok xx."

I dread Mum's response.

"Oh, darling I'm so glad to hear this Amy! I'm on my way in now. I packed another bag just in case. Oh, and Jack you and I will be having words. Mum xx."

Mum and Jack never fail to make me smile, but I certainly didn't want to be in the room when that conversation happens. Due to not having a father who is in my life, it will probably fall to Mum to have that conversation with Jack, which will be interesting because they've known each other for years; she almost sees him as the son she's never had.

chapter 13

I'm so glad to be out of hospital and recovering at home. There's nothing worse than being stuck there for days on end. Jack says that I am welcome to stay at his, but I'm not sure how I can rest given how many people come and go in that house. I barely make it through the door before collapsing on the sofa. Jack gets my bag out of the car and leaves it in my room.

After I have a nap, we facetime Jack's nieces and nephews. Mum gets my purple and blue fluffy blanket from my room. Jack gets my bag out of the car and dumps it in my room. I struggle to even take off my splints independently and need to ask Mum for help. I try to do it myself, but my body just caves in. Given how many drugs had been pumped into me the last twenty-four hours and having little to no sleep, this makes me physically and mentally drained.

My body feels so weak. Every step feels like a punch to the stomach. Mum had made sure that she had the essentials in stock before I arrived home; Maltesers, plenty of lemonade and a phone charger by the sofa. Even though in the hospital,, she seemed to be unfazed by the whole situation, I can tell she was concerned but wants to stay strong to keep us both going.

Jack stays snuggled into me the entire afternoon as we watch *The Greatest Showman* and *Moulin Rouge.* Every half an hour or so, Mum checks on us. Jack takes full advantage of this. Every time she comes in, she brings food, the best way to his heart.

I can hear her on the phone in the kitchen. "No, she's ok, exhausted but that was expected given that it's been so long since the last one. I'm just glad that we've got her home. I'll give you a call later, alright. Thanks. Amy."

Mum walks into the living room to check on me once again. "That was Amy. She just wanted to check that you're getting better and sends her love."

I am struggling to even sit up without feeling exhausted. All I want to do was sleep, but my brain doesn't seem to want to shut down. "How is she?"

Mum seems a little surprised that I'd even asked, given my current state. "She's alright, thanks, darling. She just wanted to make sure that you were on the mend."

Usually, I would tell Mum to get out whilst Jack was here, but it's nice to have the two closest people to me by my side.

"What are we going to watch next then?"

I feel like my body had let me down big time, and I'm worried how long it will take to repair. I've worked so hard for years to manage my disabilities in the best way I know how. How can something that pushes me forward also hold me back?

The following morning, I wake up feeling slightly better. Getting a decent night's sleep in my own bed definitely helped. My muscles are still slightly achy, but I'm thankfully on the mend.

"Good morning, babe. How are you feeling? Did you sleep any better being at home? xx"

I instantly smile because even when Jack is not with me, he's always so caring.

"A lot better. Thanks for everything you've done for me these past few days love you xx"

I am so lucky to have a fantastic support network that rally around me when I need them most. I switch on my TV to find reruns of *Friends*. Even though I've seen them as much as *Scrubs,* comfort TV is what I need right now. After a while, Mum comes in with a tray. On it, are two pieces of butter toast cut diagonally and a glass of apple juice. Next to the glass is a small pot that contains the tablets that I need to take.

"Good morning darling, how are you feeling?" Mum stays in my room whilst I take my medication. Mum watches me take the medication feels awkward and like I have gone back five years but can understand why she wants to check.

Since arriving home yesterday afternoon, Mum has already devised a chart of what tablet I need to take and when. Typically, I would be annoyed as I like to be in charge of my medication, and Mum can sometimes be a bit over the top with these things. However, given my current state, it's a blessing in disguise.

I feel incredibly fragile. My body has let me down once again. I'm now worried because I could have another seizure at any point. What if it happens in one of my exams? What if I have one on my own? I've fought hard not to let my disabilities control my life, but when everything is under control and I start achieving, they appear.

Getting dressed is my greatest challenge this week. I don't even bother putting on my splints. It's not like I can move far.

Doctors have told me before that having a seizure is a bit like running a marathon; after it's over, everything hurts. I open my phone to the group chat between Josh, myself, and our deputy's. They are keeping me up to date with everything that is happening.

As I'm typing, Jack arrives at the house and walks into my room and makes himself comfortable on my bed. "What are you doing?"

I want him to do something for himself this weekend as he has been by my side since I had the seizure. However, he isn't having any of it, and he cancels any plans that he did have.

"What are you doing?" he asks even though he already knows.

"Just messaging the senior team." I put my phone on my bedside cabinet that has also been host to a variety of snacks.

In my mind, I only want to be off for two weeks as I know how much revision and coursework I still have left to do. I am not sure how I will manage walking around school, as for the past week, I've barely moved. My longest walk was to the kitchen and then back to bed. I decide to put on proper clothes and take a walk around the village with Mum.

"Darling, we don't have to do this. We could always try tomorrow?"

"No, Mum! I have to do this! My disabilities can't hold me back. I need to do this to set an example."

I finally feel strong enough to go back to school. Given that my first exam is only three weeks away, I can't afford to waste any more time being at home in bed. As I walk into the main foyer, all I can hear is the overwhelming sound of applause from students and teachers alike.

Mr Perkins stands in the foyer, making sure everyone goes to their lessons, and he asks me to go and see him in his office. I walk along the main corridor and receive looks of appreciation that I'm alright.

"Amy, it's so lovely to see you. We were all so worried about you. How are you feeling?" H ushers me to his office. As we walk a lot of students send me looks of appreciation that I'm alright.

Josh is already in. his usual seat in the office and even he looks pleased to see me, which is unusual but a nice change.

"Thanks, sir, I'm feeling a lot better and ready to get back to my duties," I say.

He looks pleased but still a bit concerned. "Are you sure? I would fully understand if you still needed a few weeks. Your deputy can step in if you need her to?"

I can understand why he suggests this, but I am eager to get back to making the school a better place.

"No, sir, thanks, but I want to use this experience to show students that even when you get knocked down, it's all about getting back up and carrying on. Epilepsy never has and never will win. It just makes me stronger to keep fighting. It also encourages me to raise awareness so that people know what it's like living with this condition." At this point I'm so riled up that I'm word vomiting.

"Unfortunately, epilepsy, much like all disabilities, comes with a stigma, which we as a society need to come to terms with and then put right. Whilst recovering at home, I researched a lot about epilepsy and how it can be such a taboo subject. I'm not sure if you were aware, but a study done by the University of Liverpool found that 69 percent of teenagers asked said that they wouldn't date someone with epilepsy. Opinions need to change now, as this is not acceptable. If we don't talk about it, opinions won't change, and if opinions don't change, the stigma will never end. When I went for my RADA audition on the train, someone thought that Jack was my carer. I will never give up fighting because I know I'm incredibly fortunate having the disabilities that I have and still be able to accomplish all the amazing things I have so far. My goal is to make the acting sector more inclusive but that I know is going to be hard, so it's vital to start somewhere that is achievable in the short term."

Both Mr Perkins and Josh smile proudly.

"Amy, you are such an inspiration, and we as a school are so lucky to have you as our head girl." I've never seen Mr Perkins's face so full of joy and pride.

"We have a few things to discuss." He sits forward on his chair and opens a large red leather notebook. "So, as you are both aware, we have quite a few events that we need you to attend." He looks down at his notebook. "Firstly, we have a few open days for potential students at the school, and we need you both to attend as school representatives. Prefects will be guiding the students around the school, but what we would like you both to do is to be in the foyer at the beginning of the day so that friendly faces greet them. Oh, Amy, we were wondering if you would like to share your story with the students?"

I instantly feel an enormous sense of pride; for once, my disabilities are being used to encourage and inspire, instead of being a burden. "Sir, I would be honoured."

"Also, it has come to my attention that some prefects are not performing their duties correctly and to the standard expected. Can we just keep an eye on this when we're doing rounds around the school?"

I'm still incredibly uncomfortable about doing this as essentially, it's telling off my friends, some of whom I've known for years. Still, I had to do my role correctly, no matter how I felt about doing it.

"Now, that's out the way. Let's get on with the more important stuff. As we are now in March, we are only four months away from prom."

This sends shivers down my spine for many reasons; one, it is the most important night of the year. Two, I get to wear a stunning dress and feel like a princess.

He adds, "Now we need to come up with a theme, so I'm asking you both for suggestions?"

It's a lot of pressure ultimately deciding for an entire year group. Therefore, if they don't like it, we probably won't ever live it down.

Josh then pipes up. "I think we should have a superhero's theme. Then I can wear my Superman costume."

I wait for the laughter, but it doesn't come.

"Ok, well, that's one idea. I really appreciate your input, Josh; we will certainly take that on board." I felt that Mr Perkins has to say this but can tell by the expression on his face that this isn't what he is thinking. "Amy, do you have any ideas?"

His eyes are almost doing the talking by saying, do you have anything else, please!

I swiftly put him out of his misery. "Well, how about we do a night at the movies theme?"

Mr Perkins nods. Josh seems less than impressed. "Boring!"

"I'm sorry?" I am giving him a chance to reword his insulting response.

"Every year, I see the prom being set up. It just looks so boring and never impresses me. We have a chance this year to change that," he says.

I can understand where he's coming from to a point, but I'm not going to agree with him.

I'm sure that Mr Perkins can feel that the tension in the room is building, and he says, "Alright, alright, well, thank you both for your opinions. I will now take these ideas to the senior leadership team. We will have another meeting on Friday to finalise the theme as tickets need to go on sale next week."

As both of us are just about to stand up and go to our next lesson, Mr Perkins stops us. "Oh, yes, one more thing. It's a tradition at this school that the head boy and head girl arrive at prom together to open it to the rest of the year group."

Josh and I aren't exactly delighted at this so-called tradition. It is the first thing we've agreed on.

"So, hang on, what you're saying is I have to arrive with him. When I already have arranged to go with Jack?" I ask.

Josh says, "And you're saying that I've got to go with her when I could score way higher, no offence."

I take offence. "I'm sorry. What exactly do you mean by that?"

Josh stutters. "No, no, Amy, I didn't mean to cause any offence by what I said. Oh gosh, please forgive me. I'm just saying that you're a nice person but not really my type."

I have no plan of forgiving him anytime soon.

As neither one of us want to back down, we've both forgotten that Mr Perkins is standing in the middle of us. "Will you both just STOP IT! We have chosen you both to represent the school. Now this is one of your duties and let me remind you that the school is paying for the car."

We both look down at the floor like we were back at primary school being told off for the first time, which might actually be the case for Josh.

Josh would usually at this point suck up to Mr Perkins and say something like "ladies first," when really it is all an act. He is the biggest suck up I've ever had the displeasure of knowing. This time, he is having none of it and promptly throws his bag over his shoulder and storms out of the office.

"I guess we can now see who the bigger person is!" I say, following him out.

He stops in the corridor and turns around to face me. "I'm sorry, what did you say?"

He stands over me, trying to act tough. However, it isn't scaring me one bit,

"Oh, I think you heard me the first time!" I say.

He has that surprised look on his smug face like he is outraged that someone had the guts to speak back to him.

I say, "You think I'm scared of you? You can try and make yourself as big as you like, but it's not going to work on me."

"Do you even know who you're talking to? I can get the whole of the school to turn against you. At least I know who my dad is, unlike some people," he says whilst looking me up and down like he's so much better than me.

Everything falls so silent that for a moment I would be able to hear a pin drop.

This is all that he had on me. "Oh, go on then," I say whilst laughing, "see how far you get with a story that has nothing to do with me!"

I can see in his eyes that he's running out of comebacks.

"Well!" Suddenly, everyone in the corridor turns around to look at Josh. He has paused to allow his brain to construct a sentence and he continues. "At least I'm not SPECIAL!"

"WHAT DID YOU JUST SAY?" I'm struggling to string any sentence together as my whole body has gone into shock.

Mr Perkins is right behind Josh. He's heard everything.

"Mr Pickington, a word, now!"

He ushers Josh back into the office. There's suddenly a loud "ooh" noise from the crowd that had gathered around us, and Mr Perkins says, "And the rest of you can get to class now before I give you all detention!"

A moment later he focuses on me and asks, "Amy, are you going to be, ok? I can get someone to walk with you if you want?"

Through the office door, I can see that Josh looks full of regret of for what he has just said. I'm shaken, but I need to be strong. This isn't the first time this has happen and I doubt it will be the last.

"No, sir, thanks for the offer; I'll be ok. I guess some people still need to be educated."

The rest of the day is a bit of a blur. Miss Stevens asks me whether or not I've heard back from RADA, but I have yet to hear anything. As I make my way to the bus stop to go home, I notice that Jack was already there.

I ask, "Hey, I thought you said you were going to meet me after lesson?"

Jack stares down at the ground and gets on the bus without saying a word.

Jack isn't his usual chatty self for the entire bus journey home. I ask him a couple of times whether he's alright. He doesn't say a word. I assume that he's probably tired or someone has annoyed him; we get back to his, and he promptly picks me up and says, "We need to talk upstairs, now."

His face is emotionless whilst carrying me upstairs. We get into his bedroom; he puts me on the bed and remains standing over me. I'm scared because he's never like this with me.

"What's this I hear about prom?" His voice is quiet but very stern.

"What do you mean about prom?"

"Well, let me spell it out for you!" His face becomes more red with every word. "As I was in my last lesson just about to come and get you because that's what a good boyfriend I am. I find out that my girlfriend isn't going to prom with me, no, no, she's going with the guy that I despise the most. Seriously, I think this head girl thing has got to your head. Everyone knows that the head boy and head girl have a reputation of hooking up at the after-prom party." He suddenly started breathing very heavily and looked at me in a way I've never seen before.

He is standing over me with his arms crossed. "Oh my God, seriously? You're actually throwing this back in my face. What happened to I'll support you through anything? I can't believe that you think that I'm going to cheat on you with Josh of all people, urgh!"

"I still stand by that. It would've been nice to be told that this was happening instead of finding out from someone else. It's like you're trying to hide something, are you? I know what a suck-up Josh can be, and I don't want to lose you. After all, he's such a gentleman."

I know he's being sarcastic. Jack's opinion of Josh is the complete opposite. I can't believe that he's got zero faith in me, not cheating on him. "So, what do you want me to do? NOT GO? Jack, you're the one that was known as the player. Before me, you used to go from girl to girl, not caring about whether or not you hurt them. Which let me add, you did a lot! Anyway, since when do I have to ask your permission? I'm not hiding anything; this is one of my duties as head girl, that's all."

I can tell that I've struck a chord.

He says, "I told you the only reason that I went from girl to girl was because I didn't know how to tell you how I actually felt! So, don't you DARE through it back in my face. How would you feel if it was the other way around?"

I take a deep breath and lower my voice. "See, it hurts when someone accuses you of something that isn't true. Babe, if it were up to me, I wouldn't be going to prom with that idiot. Of course I would be hurt if you were going with someone else, but you need to understand that is one of my duties as head girl. You said that you would be supportive when I got the position, and you couldn't be prouder. So, have you changed your mind? Anyway, you didn't hear what he said?"

Jack looks at me somewhat confused.

I say, "He called me special, but not in the way that you do."

"He said what?!"

I can tell that all Jack wants to do was beat the crap out of him. Josh and Jack didn't get on before because they are polar opposites of each other, so this has definitely added fuel to the fire.

"You heard me the first time."

Jack flops on the bed next to me. "Babe, I'm so sorry. It's just all I've heard all day. I couldn't think of losing you."

I cuddle him tightly. "It's ok. I understand where you're coming from, but he's a complete idiot. If it was the other way around and I heard that you were taking someone else to prom without telling me, I'm sure you would never hear the end of it. You have to understand that even if I were single, I would never go there because my standard is so much higher than that. I do love how protective you are of me, though."

Him kissing me is all the reassurance I need to know that he's the only one for me.

"I love you. I never want to see you get hurt by anyone," he says.

I looked back at him and stared directly into his eyes. "I love you more."

"Loves?" Jenny calls whilst knocking on the door. "It's me. I heard you two shouting. I wanted to make sure that everything is ok?"

I love Jenny, but sometimes she gets involved in things that she doesn't need to.

Jack says, "Yeah, everything's fine. Thanks, Mum."

I'm so glad that he didn't tell her.

"This stays between us, ok? Which means that not even Emma can know about this." I look straight at him whilst still in his embrace. "Look. I think I've been through enough this year. What with the family and everything, so promise something that you will be there for me, please?"

I give him innocent eyes. He knows I'm serious.

"Of course, I will, you may drive me crazy sometimes, but I wouldn't have you any other way," he says.

I gesture at my frame. "Even if I didn't have that?"

"Without that, you wouldn't be the girl that I fell in love with, babe. I've never judged you on your disabilities and would never even dream too, you know that. It's part of you. I'm proud to call you my girlfriend. You're the most driven, inspiring person I've ever met. I'm the lucky one. Like I've said before, why do you think I've never had a serious relationship? All the girls I've ever dated are like here," his hand is at his chest, "but you, Amy, are here." His hand is now as high as he can possibly reach.

My smile grows so big that my mouth starts to hurt as I kiss him passionately. All I've wanted my whole life is someone who loves me for me. Sometimes dreams really do come true.

chapter 14

Having still heard nothing back from RADA, I start wondering whether the call in the hospital was from them, but I've completely forgotten to grill Jack about the call he wouldn't tell me about. I lay on my bed trying to not to think about the worst-case scenario which is where my brain usually automatically goes. I briefly think about getting in touch with them, but surely that sounds a bit desperate. Also, considering how the first half of my audition went, it probably isn't the best idea. The more time that goes on, the less hope I've got of actually getting a place. Suddenly, my phone lights up. It's blocked number which usually I don't answer. However, I have a strange feeling that this was going to be different.

"Hello?" I'm unsure what else to say.

"Good morning, is that Amy?" The voice is very professional.

I try to reciprocate as best I can but fail miserably as nerves get the better of me. "Speaking."

"Hello Amy, it's Nicole from RADA."

My muscles tense up. "Oh, hello Nicole, how are you? It's lovely to hear from you."

"Very well, thanks, Amy. Are you feeling better now? I heard that you were in the hospital. I'm so sorry to hear this."

I'm touched that she's asked. "Yes, I am, thank you. I think it was just a medication issue." I don't want to give her too many details.

"Well, I'm glad to hear this. I hope that everything is now sorted or at the very least in the process."

I just want her to get to the point of the call; the wait is killing me.

"Anyway, Amy, once again, thanks for auditioning with us; it was such a pleasure to meet you."

At this point, I'm mentally preparing myself for this to go one of two ways.

"So, Amy, we felt that your audition was so empowering. We were in awe of your determination to chase your dreams. It's definitely an audition that has stuck with the whole of the panel."

I smile at this but don't reply.

She continues, "As you know, the competition to get into RADA is incredibly tough. We only have thirty places within the programme, so I regret to inform you that you've been unsuccessful this time. However, we do hope that you will come and audition for us again in September."

I don't hear the rest of what she said as my whole body goes numb. My hands start shaking. I struggle to keep hold of the phone. I have to grab onto my frame with the other hand as I am so afraid that my legs are going to collapse.

After what feels like hours, I manage to compose myself to give a response. "Well, I appreciate the opportunity to audition for your school and look forward to seeing you in September."

Jack, unfortunately, walks in at the wrong moment. "Oh my god, babe! You got in. I knew you would; you're amazing. Let's go and celebrate."

I grab onto his hand, staring at the wall in utter shock. The phone falls to the floor as I stare at the wall in a state of shock. "No, babe, I didn't, I didn't get a place."

Saying it causes me to break down. Jack slumps onto the bed next to me. His shoulders drop as he puts his arm around me. "I'm so sorry, babe. I'm struggling to understand you when you sound like a dog howling."

I start laughing and crying simultaneously, but because I'm laughing, it just makes me cry even more. What a vicious circle.

Jack puts both his arms around me as I dropped my head into his elbow and cry.

He says, "It's going to be ok; I promise. You can have

another shot next year. By then, you'll be even better. They'll definitely regret not accepting you the first time."

Trying my best to compose myself, I say, "I know my audition wasn't perfect, but I thought I had a shot at getting a place. I don't understand. What am I meant to do now?"

Jack also seems lost for words and keeps stroking my back to try and console me.

Jenny bursts through the door. "What's wrong? Amy darling."

She wraps her arms around me and holds me tightly. I think Jack mouths what's happened; I don't think I could've explained it again.

"Amy, look at me." She holds onto my shoulders. "I promise you this is going to be ok. Sometimes in life, we have to lose ourselves to find the best version of ourselves."

There are only three weeks to go until my first exam and only six until prom. I am starting to wonder if somehow, I could magic up more hours in the day as time was running out and fast. My lessons are revision and exam prep; it's scary how close we are to the end. Josh and I have several meetings with Mr Perkins to finalise the details for prom. In the end, we go with "A Night at the Movies Theme."

Jack and my relationship has been a bit on the rocks, which hasn't helped. Some days he's really supportive, and other's he hardly spoke to me. I'm sure I don't improve the situation by asking what's wrong fifty times a day! I feel like we need to go to the park and have a chat but fear that this could make things worse.

We arrive home one afternoon. Jack carries me upstairs as we both had so much revision to do. "We need to talk in your room," he says as he carries me through and places me on my bed.

"Are you ok?" I ask.

He is acting as if something is bottling up inside him and about to explode.

"Look, I've been thinking about this for a while, and there's no easy way to say this. We are both so busy at the minute, amazing things are happening for both of us, but that doesn't leave a lot of time for us." His face has changed entirely. He is expressionless, like he has rehearsed this beforehand.

"So, what are you saying? Are you breaking up with me?" My lips start to wobble, tears stream down my face, and I can feel snot trickling from my nose.

"No, I'm not exactly saying break up as such."

"So, what are you saying?" I snap.

He looks down at the floor. "I'm just saying that maybe we should give each other some space. We have no idea what is going to happen over the next couple of months. Amy, I love you; I love you so much. You're an incredible person and such an amazing light for me. However, you need to do what you got to do, and so do I. I know this sucks to hear, and trust me, it's not any easier saying it, but I've realised that I need to work out some things by myself. I promise you; you haven't done anything wrong, and I'm not disappearing off with anyone else."

I can feel myself grabbing onto his arms and trying to wake myself up like it's some dream.

"I love you too, Jack. We don't have to do this. I know I've been crazy busy. I will always find time for you, please, Jack, I love you."

He doesn't answer.

"Jack, why now? This is probably the worse time to do this."

He takes a slight pause. "Look, what we've been through the past five months has been quite intense. Couples who have been together for years don't have this much drama. I promised myself that I would be here for you no matter what, and that is still true. I just feel that we are becoming further and further apart. I think this is the best thing to do."

"So, what are you saying? I'm drama? I can't control the things that my family do! I also can't help having a seizure. You said you would always be there for me! I guess you've now changed your mind." Even though my voice has now got so much louder, Jack somehow manages to stay calm.

"I know you can't, and trust me, this is not why I am doing this. Sometimes you make yourself believe that you're so happy, but soon you realise that you're depriving your own dreams. I really want to go to university, study law and hopefully one day become a lawyer. Even though I support all your dreams and find it so attractive how driven you are, I need to work out what I want as well."

He's right. I feel awful that for the past year I've been so selfish.

"We are both so young and have the rest of our lives to figure this out. The one thing that will never change is how I feel about you. You're smart, funny, and absolutely gorgeous," he says.

I've never really supported Jack's dreams because I've been so focused on my own dreams.

He says, "Amy, I can't even begin to explain how much I love you. I'll still be your best friend. Whatever happens, I will be here for you, but right now, I need to focus on what's best for me and then who knows? I haven't stopped loving you, and I don't think I ever will, but right now, I can't be with you."

I'm losing the best thing in my life. "Can I ask you a question?"

He looks up at me. "Anything Amy."

I don't like him calling me by my actual name. "If I stayed here and we went to the same college, would you still do this?"

He looks sympathetic. "Well, maybe not, but then you wouldn't be the person that I fell in love with. I love you that much that I want you to chase your dreams, so I need to set you free."

"I don't understand, Jack. I didn't get into RADA." Saying this causes even more pain. "I have no idea what I'm going to do next year. Why can't we figure this out together?" I'm in a no-win situation. "Why can't we stay together for the summer because I don't really have any plans yet?"

I know this isn't going to work, but it's my last attempt to try and change his mind. Jack just looks at me knowing that this is probably the worst thing we could do.

"Amy, you know we would just be putting off the inevitable. If we do it now, we both have a chance to get used to not being together before we chase our dreams. I'm so sorry. I wish there were a way that we could work this out together. Unfortunately, this is the way it has to be. I will never stop loving you. I just can't be with you right now."

Jack kisses me for the last time.

I manage to say, "Ok, well, I guess it's best that I move back home so that we have some real-time apart. Jack, I love you, and I know I won't ever stop."

My body feels limp as we go into my room and packed up my suitcase to go back to Mum's.

I say, "I can't believe this is it. I never thought that it would come to this."

Someone has ripped my heart out and stomped on it.

Jack stands in the doorway, holding my suitcase to put by the top of the stairs. He puts it down and then grabs onto both my hands. "Look, I love you too so much. Everything I've said to you is true, but I just don't think I can be fully committed to this relationship right now. I need to focus on myself for a while. I knew this would hurt you, and believe me when I say this; it's not any easier doing it. I know it sucks, but sometimes the hardest thing to do is the right thing to do."

I can tell this is hurting him, but he's trying to be strong for both of us.

"Ok." I say and text my mum to come get me, knowing she'll be concerned, but I'm not ready to put in writing what just happened.

Within minutes Mum knocks on Jack's door. I suddenly realise that Jenny was downstairs and isn't yet aware of what had happened. Jenny and Mum look at each other, confused.

"What's going on?" Mum looks worried as I'm sure she can tell that I've been crying. Jack comes to sit next to me on the sofa; he grabs hold of my hand, part of me wants to grab on tightly, and part wants to let go immediately.

Jack takes a deep breath. "We have something to tell you."

Both Jenny and Mum took a deep breath and Mum says, "Oh my God, you're pregnant!"

I'm a little shocked at the response. "No, no!" I look at Jack. "We have decided," I choke up, "to take a break from each other."

Jenny clears her throat. "I don't understand. Why? After

everything we've done for you! We let you stay here rent-free, we made sure you were safe. Even after your seizure, we said that you could stay here if you needed to. How could you do this to my—"

I start to cry even more because I know how much this has hurt Jenny, but her son is to blame for this, not me!

Jack cuts her off abruptly. "Mum! Stop it! This was a mutual decision."

I look straight at him, and he rephrases it. "Well, actually, it was mainly me. Look, we're both so young that we have the rest of our lives to figure this out." He gives me a half-smile.

Jack focuses on my mum. "I cannot tell you how much I love your daughter. She's incredible and an amazing light, but this is the best thing for us right now. I also have a lot of figuring out to do. I wish I were like Amy, where I knew exactly where I wanted to go in life. However, the truth is I don't." He chuckles. "I know for years I've said about how I want to go travelling, but the truth is the only reason why I want to do that is that I have no idea what else I want to do. The future terrifies me, and I was planning to use travelling as an escape. I don't want to make promises to Amy that I can't keep."

I tell Jenny, "I still absolutely adore your son a lot and would never want to see any harm done to him. Right now, it's tough to be together, and even though it hurts, we both know this is the right decision."

I immediately burst into floods of tears. Mum wraps her arms around me and holds me tight.

Mum says to Jenny, "I think we need to support the kid's decision."

I'm so thankful that at one least of them was supportive. Jack only lives around the corner from us, but Mum still brought the car as she was probably in a panic. When we go outside, Jack stands by the car and wraps his arms around me. How can something feel both reassuring and heart wrenching at the same time? As we drive away, I turn to look out of the rear window. The love of my life is now a dot in the distance.

chapter 15

The weekend goes by in a big blur. I've always read those posts about breakups and how you should go thirty days without contacting each other. How do you do this, though, when it's your best friend, and for years you've spoken every day? I feel broken and unsure how I will ever put myself back together.

Josie and Emma stay around mine all weekend to keep me company. If they weren't there, I would for sure be ringing him or, even worse, inviting him over.

"Hun, I know right now it feels like your whole world has fallen apart but trust me, it will get better. Do you remember my ex, Martin?" Josie and Martin are the first official couple in our friendship group back in Year 10. Unfortunately, when they broke up, they couldn't stand to be around each other, so he was sort of fazed out of the group. "When we broke up, I thought my whole world had ended, but now looking back, it was one of the best things that happened to me."

"Josie, I get that, but you and Martin don't speak to each other at all anymore. I can't imagine Jack not being in my life," I say as I sob on her shoulder.

Mum does her best to try and ease the pain. "Darling, it's going to be alright. Right now, you both need some time and space. I know it feels like your world has fallen apart right now, but I can promise that this is only the beginning of your journey. Yours and Jack's relationship was very serious very quickly. Amy, you need to remember that you're both so young who knows what the future holds. Josie, Emma, tea?"

Within seconds, she promptly comes back into my room with two bucket-sized mugs of tea for my girls. Mum's cups of tea are the best.

"Mum, I've lost the love of my life. The person who normally picks me up from being hurt and tells me that everything going to be alright. I know it was the right decision, but it doesn't make it any easier."

She takes a breath and holds onto my hand. "Darling, before your dad changed, we were madly in love. We met when we were eighteen and spent so many evenings driving around for hours, talking about how we were going to change the world." Mum's eyes light up. This is something I've never seen before; Mum is happy talking about my sperm donor.

"Jo, that was beautiful." Emma says. Her love life has been more of a car crash than mine. "I just hope that I can find someone who isn't an idiot."

"Mum, you never really talk about him in this way," I say, and she cups my cheek.

"I guess I've had to grieve over him like he's died, which to me he has." There is suddenly an uncomfortable silence. "Girls, you're all still so young, don't worry. It will happen when the time is right and trust me, it will be worth the wait. Yes, Emma, I've heard about some of the boys you go out with; I expect more from you. Any man should think that he is the luckiest man in the world if he ends up with any of you three."

She sighs and says, "I know, darling, that's because I sometimes find it hard to remember what a good man he was before. I want you to realise that even if now it feels like your whole world has fallen apart, things will get better. You won't feel this pain forever, I promise. I know Jack didn't want to hurt you, but he realised that he had to do what was best for him right now. I'm sure that this decision wasn't easy for him to make. He's probably been thinking about it for a long time. If I could wave a magic wand to make it better, I would. He's done it now because he cares about you so much and only wants the best for you, even if you can't see it that way right now. Now drink your tea before it goes cold."

There are silent and taking in every word that Mum is

saying. It is almost as if they are taking mental notes.

I smile. "Mum, I'm sorry that I left to go to Jack's, but at that time, I didn't know what else to do. You threw a lot of information at me at once, and I needed to escape the situation to process it all."

"I don't blame you because, at your age, I would've done the same thing."

I look at my phone, and his name lights up. I ask Josie, "What do I do?"

She immediately takes the phone off me.

"Just keep quiet." As she answers it and puts it on speaker, she says, "Hey Jack, what's up? Amy's in the toilet." She could've said anything, but she chose to say that.

"Oh, could you ask her to call me back, Emma, please?" She shakes her head vigorously, as she knows any second, I'm going to say something.

"To be honest, Jack, I don't think the best idea right now. Amy's hurting a lot, and I think her speaking to you would just make the situation worse. I'll let her know you've called, bye." She throws my phone back at me. "He truly seems heartbroken. I feel awful. You two can't speak to each other right now. You hear me? No phone calls, texts, DM'S nothing, for now anyways. It's for the best."

"I wish I had friends like you ladies when I was younger," Mum says. "I remember my first boyfriend years before I met Amy's father. Anyway, he broke up with me because he wanted to get with my friend instead. The night that it happened, I remember all I did was listen to 'Nothing Compares 2 U" by Sinéad O'Connor on repeat. It drove your grandparents nuts, oh just one thing?"

She pauses. I panic.

"You two didn't, you know?" she asks.

Josie and Emma stare straight at their phones; this is awkward.

"No, Mum, Jenny made sure that we slept in different rooms, and whenever we were in his room, we had to keep the door open."

Mum looks reassured. "Ok good, because I definitely don't want grandchildren quite yet."

I put an arm around her shoulder. "Don't worry. I want to have a career first."

It would be lovely to have children one day, but I need to make sure that it's with the right man. Due to my disabilities, I need to know that I can fully trust a partner before I even think about having children.

For the first time in seven years, I have to get on the bus by myself. Whilst walking to the bus stop, I dread seeing Jack. I stand at the opposite end of the bus stop to him and keep my earphones in, struggling to keep it together. I can tell that he's looking over at me every few minutes, but I continue to stare down at my phone to hide the pain.

As I walk into school, I can tell everyone already knows.

As I make my way through the foyer, all I get are sympathising looks. I have a meeting with Mr Perkins to discuss the relevant issues concerning the school; it's scary to think that we only have a couple of these meetings left before going on study leave. I have been thinking a lot lately about what I'm going to do between now and September when my RADA reaudition is. Mum suggested sending out CVs to local theatres and drama groups to get more experience and knowledge about the sector.

My lessons go by in a blur. I feel drained and my mind is only focused on one thing. I make sure that I made enough notes as I'm in no mental state to actually to remember anything. I try my hardest to avoid Jack all day. I know seeing him will be too painful. This goes well until the final bell. I walk out of the classroom and he's walking towards me. I think he's coming to speak to me, but instead, he just walks on past. It's like someone plunges a dagger into my heart repeatedly. All I want to do was cry.

To make things worse, I also have a prefect meeting after school whereby Josh and I have to sit in a room and listen to the other prefects moan about everything wrong with the school. Throughout this year, Josh and I have definitely had our ups and downs, and he isn't my perfect match; however, because we've spent so much time together, I've seen several sides to him. Finally, the meeting was over, and I only had twenty minutes to get the late bus.

He stops me. "Amy, how are you getting home?"

"Oh, I'm getting the late bus. Why?"

Smiling, he says, "Well, if you want, I'm sure my dad can give you a lift."

I can't believe Josh Pickington is actually offering to do something nice for someone else without a teacher being present. True to his word, he walks with me out of school and whilst his dad folds up my frame and puts it in the boot, Josh helps me get in the back of the BMW. The car's interior has black leather heated seats and what looks like an IPAD on the dashboard.

His dad is very friendly and polite. "So, have you got your dress yet?"

I am surprised that the school is paying for the car. However, given that his dad is one of the school's governors, it's incredibly useful, although he doesn't attend any events or meetings at school. It seems that he's actually taking an interest in me without trying to gain something for once.

I smile. "Yes, I have; it's a navy dress with sequins all over it. It's definitely the nicest thing I've ever owned."

I loved my dress so much, and it makes me feel like an actual princess. Jack had bought the corresponding tie so that might be a bit awkward.

"Well, thank you for that. I will make sure that my tailor gets the same shade of blue with my tux, just so we look amazing for the photos. Not that we wouldn't look amazing without coordinating colours," Josh says.

As we arrive along my road, many of the neighbours have

their noses pressed against their window, probably because they've never seen such a nice car.

"Well, thanks for the lift home." Josh gets my frame out of the boat and puts it by the car door.

"It's my absolute pleasure, Amy. If you ever need a lift again, don't hesitate to ask. I would be more than happy to help. Have a delightful evening." His smile is infectious.

"Well, I keep that in mind. Thanks once again, see you tomorrow."

Being a gentleman, he makes sure that I get into my house before leaving.

As I come in the door, Mum is at the bottom of the stairs looking out the front window with a confused expression. "Who was that? In that nice car?"

"That's Josh, the head boy." I am about to say about that he came over for a film night at Christmas but then remember that I was living at Jack's at the time. "We had a meeting after school, and he offered to drop me off. So that I didn't have to get the bus."

I go through to my room, drop my bag on the floor and then start to work through the mountain of homework and revision I have.

Just as I was getting into the swing of things, I receive a text from Josh.

"Hey, have you got any plans for next Tuesday? I don't believe we have many meetings. How do you fancy going and getting some ice cream? I can pick you up if you'd like around 4ish?"

I have a lump in my throat; it feels like I'm cheating on Jack. Although he didn't actually mention the word date, so technically I wouldn't be doing anything wrong. Besides, Jack and I have been broken up for a few weeks, I can't wait forever.

"Sure. I'd love that"

True to his word, Josh arrives ready to pick me up the next day. While I am making sure I have everything before I left, Mum was standing by the front window. She asks, "Why is there a guy standing outside holding a car door open?"

"Oh, that's Josh's driver. We're going out for some ice cream."

She looks at me, concerned. Just as I'm about to walk out the door, I explain. "No, Mum, it's not what it looks like. We need to discuss some things for prom."

"Ok, well, just be careful. It's only been a few weeks, and I'm sure if Jack knew what you were doing, he wouldn't be happy."

Technically, I'm not doing anything wrong because we are just friends. I definitely don't see Josh in any other way whatsoever.

As I'm walking down my path, Josh appears from the other side of the car to greet me whilst his driver holds the door open. After making sure that I'm safely in the car, Josh attempts to fold up my frame to put in the boot.

"Forgive me, I should probably know this, but Amy, how

do you collapse your frame?" Josh seems almost embarrassed that he doesn't already know this.

"Oh, yeah, sorry. Don't worry about it. You've just got two push the two buttons on either side of the frame, and then it will start to collapse."

After several attempts, Josh manages to fold it up and put it in the car's boot.

"Well, it's such a pleasure to have the most delightful company," he says. Even after a couple of months of working together, I'm still not used to how well-spoken he is.

Being the gentlemen he is, Josh holds the door open for me once we arrive at the diner. Inside it's like one of those classic American diners that you see in the movies. There are brightly coloured leather booths against the windows and those metal straws containers.

Vintage jukeboxes are on each table where you can select a specific song that then gets played in the restaurant. Shortly after we sit, a waitress takes our orders. She looks like her smile is glued to her face.

"Hey, what can I get you?" She pulls her notepad out of her apron and one of those small pencils.

I decide to go for a chocolate ice cream sundae with whipped cream on top. I don't know if this is the best idea as I need to fit in my prom dress in a few weeks. Josh decides to go for a waffle sundae with extra whipped cream. He definitely can eat anything he wants and still look amazing.

"So, I was just wondering, what made you invite me out

for ice cream?" I am slightly suspicious as it's entirely out of the blue.

"Well, I want to get to know my date for the prom a bit better, and also I want to apologise for the way I've acted towards you. I am a nice guy, or at least I try to be. Amy, you have my sincerest condolences for not getting into RADA. It's their loss and not yours."

It's nice he's taking an interest in my life, given how self-centred he appears to be sometimes.

"Well, thank you. I'm trying my best to be optimistic. There's always a chance next year. So, what are your plans after finishing school?" I probably should know this as I've seen him nearly every school day since September.

"Well, depending on my final grades, I hope to go to King's College in London to study medicine. So, year after next, hopefully, we will be seeing a lot of each other, which will be nice as I know you'll get into RADA again."

I admire how optimistic he is; I wish I had the same enthusiasm.

Not long after our desserts arrive, and the waitress gives us both one of those really long spoons. "Do you mind if I move this just, it's blocking the aisle?" She points to my frame, which by now I'm very much used to. She moves one of the chairs on the table opposite and replaces it with my frame. "Thank you so much." She almost seemed apologetic.

"So, how are you doing?" Josh asks and I know exactly

what he's referring to. I'm honestly surprised that it hasn't come up sooner.

"I'm ok. I mean, I'm devasted that it didn't work out, but we're both on completely different paths at the moment." I don't want to show how much pain I'm in and also want to keep some things private between Jack and me. "Maybe it's for the best, but I really do miss him."

"Well, you never know what the future holds, but if you need anything, then I'm here."

"Well, thanks, I'll definitely keep that in mind."

The waitress came over with the bill and Josh insists on paying. "No, no, it was my invitation, please allow me."

I don't want to give in that easily. "Don't worry. I can pay for my half at least, please?"

"I'm very old fashioned anyway, so please allow me."

chapter 16

I totally forget that Josh's driver has been waiting for us this whole time and only realise when he gets back out of the car to open the doors for us, and we get in. The driver has already turned on the air con as it was one of the hottest days of the year.

"Where are we driving to, sir?" he asks as the driver look in the rear-view mirror at Josh.

"Um, Sebastian, could you just drive around the neighbourhood for a while, please? If that's ok, Amy?" He smiles at me.

Even though I should have probably said I have to get home due to the amount of coursework and revision I have, I don't want this to end weirdly.

Josh looks at me. " So, Amy, I must ask, even though I probably know the answer already, what was your first impression of me?"

I have to think about how to word this correctly as I don't want to offend Josh. "Well, in my defence, I didn't really know you before you were awarded head boy."

"Don't worry, Amy, I can handle it." He is smiling as if he knows what's coming next.

I'm very hesitant, but I have to be honest. "Then when we had our first meeting, I thought you were some know-it-all's posh boy."

He chuckles.

I continue, "After we had that argument, I wasn't sure how we were going to get through the year without killing each other!"

He laughs. There is a moment's pause. "And now?"

Do I tell him the truth? What about Jack? Why should I be worried about Jack when we're not even together anymore?

"But you know what, Josh, you're not actually all bad." I realise how lame my answer is and instantly regret it.

"Not all bad?" He nods. Suddenly, his lips are pressed against mine.

This is amazing; I can't believe this is happening. Somehow my mind is still on Jack. One of Josh's hands is on my cheek and the other on my back; my senses have taken over. I immediately snap back to reality.

He looks at me. "I'm so sorry I'm such an idiot. I don't know what came over me."

I am still looking at him, slightly confused but can't wipe the smile off my face.

"Hang on, just let me try something." I put my hands on each side of his face. The feeling is back, and it is more intense. I pull him closer and get lost in the moment.

A knock at the window interrupts us.

Josie and Emma are standing right there, outside my house. I'm busted.

"I should probably go," I say, letting go of Josh.

He exits the car to get my frame out of the boot.

I whisper in his ear, "Can't wait for the next one," even though I knew the girls are watching. I walk to the door. I've done nothing wrong in my head, but somehow, I know I'm about to get a lecture.

As I reach into my bag for my keys, I look back at Josie and Emma. "Cup of tea?" \

Josie chuckles. "Oh honey, I think we're going to need something stronger than that".

Thankfully Mum is at work and will be for the next few hours.

I place three tea bags in our large mugs, then use a tea towel to steady the bottom of the kettle whilst I used my better hand to pour the water into the mugs. We all go through to the living room as Josie carries my cup in.

"So, what are you two doing here anyway?" I ask as I make myself comfy on the sofa.

"Well, we wanted to see how you were doing, but by the looks of it, you've obviously moved on already/" Josie grins uncontrollably. "What were you thinking?"

I take a sip of my tea. "Ok, I know this is not like me at all. However, he invited me out for ice cream."

Josie interrupts, "So a date?"

"No, as friends," I say.

Emma then pipes up. "Well, I don't know about you, Josie, but when I invite my friends out for ice cream, I don't say goodbye by sticking my tongue down their throat!"

"Ok, I know what it looks like, but sometimes when you're heartbroken, you do stupid stuff. Plus, we have no idea what Jack is up to at the moment. For all, we know he could have three or four girls on the go." Even as these words are falling out my mouth, I know this definitely isn't a good enough reason.

"Yeah, that must have been really hard! In all seriousness, this can't get back to Jack. It will only make things worse." Josie is having none of this. "Amy, seriously? The head boy and head girl have just made out. This is going to be the gossip of the year! I saw Jack in town the other day, and he wasn't his usual happy self. He said to me that he's never felt the way he feels about you with anyone else and certainly misses you. Amy, he doesn't love you as his girlfriend but also you are his best friend."

It isn't helpful knowing that Jack isn't dealing with the breakup well, even though he was the one who wanted the breakup in the first place. Still, they are right; this would be probably the best gossip the year have heard all year.

"Plus, remember how you both really didn't like each other at the start, and now all of a sudden, you're all over each other. Everyone loves an enemy to lover's story. The thing that you have to work out now is damage control." Josie says and I look at Josie, puzzled because I'm not entirely sure what she means. "Think about it. You and Jack have just broken up."

"It's been a while," I say.

"As I was saying, you and Jack have been best friends for years and have now dated. It didn't work out for various reasons, which I'm not even entirely sure about, but that's not my business. Now you've kissed the guy who he hated the most because of how much you were together. Even though you are technically single and allowed to do what or whoever you like, Jack is still your best friend. Amy, I don't think you realise how much this will hurt him. He will be heartbroken."

"So, what shall I do? I don't want to hurt him. Things are so complicated between us right now and it will only make things worse." I know the answer before I even ask the question.

"Well, the question is, how do you feel about him? Was it just a stupid mistake and a moment of misjudgement, or do you actually have feelings for him?" Josie asks.

"I don't know. He's a nice guy, but that's it." I can't work out in my head the right answer.

"Well, maybe, that's your answer. If you liked him, then you would be smiling and wanting to give it a shot, but you're not. You're more worried about what Jack's going to think. We all make mistakes. Now all you can do is hope he forgives you."

"So, what do I do?" I already know the answer but don't want to admit it.

In unison they say, "You need to speak to Jack." They smile at each other, and Emma then carries on, "Now before word gets around. This can't be done over the phone; this has to be done in person with just you two."

They are right; this isn't going to be pretty.

There were only a few rings until I hear Jack's calm hello.

"Hey, are you doing anything?" I really don't want to do this, but I also don't want to hurt him even more than I already had.

"Um, no, what's up?"

I want to tell him there and then, but it definitely isn't right.

"Are you able to come over? We need to talk."

His voice suddenly changes into a panic. "Are you ok? What's wrong? What do you need?"

"Just get here when you can."

Josie and Emma get up from the sofa.

Emma says, "I think we're going to leave you two to it, but text us if you need us. Whatever happens, we'll be here for you."

After they leave, I am even more nervous, my hands shake, and my body tenses. I know I can't put this off any longer. Jack will be here any minute, and I have to own up to one of the worst things I've ever done. How can just a moment of misjudgement have the potential to cause so much damage?

chapter 17

Within minutes Jack arrives. I take a deep breath and open the door. I can tell that he has run here.

Still heavily breathing, he asks, "What's wrong? Are you ok? Amy, you're starting to worry me!"

"I think you should come in." Somehow, I manage to keep myself composed; I'm not sure how I didn't make it into RADA! Jack walks into the living room and I ask, "Can I get a drink or anything?"

I'm stalling.

"Um, no, I'm good. What's going on? Amy, are you ok?"

"There's something you need to know. So, where do I start?" I'm trying to work out how I can word this. "Josh, like the rest of the school, found out about the break-up. He was really supportive, and he's actually a really nice guy. Anyway, he invited me out for ice cream."

Jack clenches his fists, but his face remains unreadable. "I still can't stand that guy. He's the biggest stuck-up idiot."

His anger isn't making this any easier.

I hold both his hands. "Jack, I love you; I only did this because I love you so much, I was—no—I *am* still heartbroken. I thought I'd lost you."

Jack lets go. "Amy, I know you kissed him. One of the boys from football saw you kissing outside the house and texted me."

I'm in total shock and wanted to know immediately exactly who it was. "Then why aren't you angry?"

"Well, the truth is I've also got something I need to confess. So, you know when I'd phoned you the other day and Emma picked up?"

I'm petrified as to what was coming next.

"Well, there's something I needed to tell you." He holds onto both my hands. "I've made the biggest mistake. So, the night before I went to a party and Beth was there, one thing led to another and suddenly—"

"DON'T TELL ME YOU GOT BACK WITH HER? I wasn't the one who wanted to break up! Now you've done this! Was it just a kiss?"

Beth and Jack have been on and off for years. She was his first time, and I don't think he's ever let that go.

"So, you're saying it's my fault! I know I wanted a break from us, but I didn't expect you to kiss somebody else. I needed some support, and she was there. Amy I don't think you understand how much you've hurt me."

"Don't you dare put this on me! You know how much I hate her for how she's treated you over the years, and you panda to it! I'm sure she was there to cater to your every need. Answer the question, did anything else happen between you two? Tell me the truth, or I won't be able to trust you ever again."

"It was an accident."

"No, an accident is when I fall over, or an accident is when you damage your foot playing football. Sleeping with someone is not an accident. You knew this would hurt me and you did it anyway. Get out of my house now!" I storm to the front door as fast as my feet can take me.

"Amy, wait! Let's talk about this! We've both made mistakes in the last week that we regret. Can't we just move past this?"

He's trying to hold my hands as he knows the warmth of his touch gets to me.

Immediately I pull back. "Oh, I'm sure she was, I bet you loved every minute. Don't you dare put this all one me. I want you to leave now."

I swing open the door.

"No, baby, let's talk about this!"

"Don't baby me! I'm sure she was a great shoulder cry to on whilst you were sticking your tongue down her throat. I know why you broke up with me. I'm too much work. Yeah, you'd rather have someone who needs to take care of you.

You wanted to get back to just kissing girls and not having to put in the work of being in a relationship."

"Amy, if you were only thinking of me whilst you were kissing that stuck up idiot, then it obviously wasn't a good kiss!"

"Were you drunk?"

"No, I had a couple at the party, but I definitely wasn't drunk, and what about my track record? Why do you always ask me that? Don't act like you're innocent in all of this, so stop acting like you've done nothing wrong."

"So, you slept with her sober? Plus, I have to, you're a terrible drunk. Remember what happened at the Halloween party?" I immediately regret saying this.

"I thought you'd forgiven me for that. Which is the whole reason that we are together? Or is this a big joke to you. Yeah, that's it. Our whole relationship was about you? I love you; you know I do, but you can be hard work." I don't think I've ever been this angry at him. "Ok, you want to go there. If I'm such hard work, then why did you say you'll support me through anything?"

"I'm done! I'll guess I'll see you in a couple of weeks."

"WAIT! I wasn't the one that wanted to break up. Jack, this was your decision. Trust me, that kiss meant nothing. What you've done has broken me!"

"Again, all about you! I didn't break up with you because I don't love you anymore. I did it because it was too hard to be together. Amy, you've crushed me, I gave you everything, and I feel like you have thrown it back in my face. I've been revising so hard, and one of the main reasons was that I wanted to make you proud, but obviously, you had different priorities. See you around. Yes, I've made a huge mistake and if I could go back and undo it I would. She means nothing to me." He walks out and doesn't look back.

As soon as the door closes, I immediately burst into tears, shaking with anger. It's amazing how you can love someone so much but don't want them anywhere near you at the same time.

I reach for my phone, *"He slept with Beth. I guess once a player, always a player".*

Within minutes the girls are at the door. "He did what!" they exclaim as they walk into the house. They both look absolutely furious.

Josie says, "Why the hell did he do that for? Was he even sorry? I knew he was a player. It just shows you how quickly he's reverted back to his old ways. What an idiot, please don't tell me you're still considering giving him another chance?"

"The thought of them two doing that sickens me but, I still love him," I say.

The girls are not impressed.

Josie puts her arm around me. "Amy, no, you can't. He has completely betrayed your trust, and for what? An ugly girl who is nowhere near your standard. I know you love Jack, but you don't deserve to be treated in this way at all."

chapter 18

Even though I'm still hurting from everything that happened over the weekend, I have to put it all to the back of my mind. I have eight exams this week, and the nerves have already kicked in. Monday morning comes around far too quickly; I am filled with nerves. Due to my medical needs and the fact it will be hard for my frame to fit in the exam hall, I'm using Mr Perkins's office. This actually makes me relax a bit as I've already spent so much time in here this year anyway. I'm also able to use a laptop and am given extra time, which I plan to use to double-check my answers to make sure that they're the best they can be. I've always wanted to make sure that I'm nottreated any different to anyone else just because I've got a disability. Still, the extra time definitely helps when I'm taking the most important exams of my life so far.

On Wednesday is one of the most crucial exams in my whole schedule, my English exam. If I don't get this right, I can kiss RADA goodbye. Thankfully I make sure that I do the extra prep for this exam and attend additional revision classes held by teachers after school. I do everything I can within the exam and feel emotionally and physically exhausted from the sheer concentration I have to endure. Now I just have to nail my English literature exam and hope it's been enough. A lot is riding on passing these exams. Somehow, I manage to block out all of these doubts and solely focused on what I need to do to the best of my ability.

Two years of preparation and working as hard as I possibly could is now in the hands of fate and the exam boards.

There are just two weeks to go until prom. I'm nervous and excited which isn't a good mix when you've got cerebral palsy. Thankfully I already have everything organised. Somehow I blocked out throughout exams week the drama that was happening with Josh and Jack. Unfortunately, now I've got a few things to deal with. How do I feel about Josh? Can Jack and I really go back to the way we were?

I have mixed emotions about finishing school. On the one hand, I'm so excited to be free finally. This year has been filled with amazing highs and crushing lows, none of which I could have predicted. I am extremely nervous about leaving school because for seven years it's been somewhere that I feel I can be myself and have the greatest support network anyone could wish for. Will I be able to cope without not seeing the girls every day? Having to make decisions about my future scares me; I don't know where I will be in a year. I've proved to myself how strong I can be. Just because I've got disabilities, I can put my mind to anything I want to.

All of us are in school today for the final time and to say goodbye to the school that had given us all so much over the past seven years. As I walk through the main gates for the last time, I have an overwhelming sense of anxiety; what is next for me? Will I be able to get a job while I'm waiting to reapply for RADA? For years I've had it all planned out and now when it's crucial to have a plan, I've got nothing.

I head through the foyer with Emma and Josie, hoping nobody knows about Jack and me. I am so caught up in my own world that I barely a young girl using crutches standing in front of me. She seems nervous as if she wants to tell me something but is unsure how.

"Hi, how are you?" I ask, hoping that this would make her feel a bit more at ease.

"Amy, hi, you don't know me. I've just started as I've finally been accepted into mainstream school. I just wanted to say thank you. You're my inspiration. Walking into a new school and seeing that the head girl has a disability is so exciting. Thank you, you've given me hope."

I don't know what to say. This whole year I've been so focused on making that all voices get heard no matter who you are. I just hope this is the start of real change.

"Wow, thank you!" Whilst hugging her, I add, "I'll make

sure to look out for you as head girl in five years."

She is jumping around in excitement, so I decide to join her whilst holding on to my frame.

"If you ever need to talk to someone about having a disability. Here you go." I put my number in her phone and then walk to tutor.

"Amy, I don't get how you have can be so confident. I would love to be like you," she says.

I am almost in tears as for the last seven years I've been working hard to make sure that my disabilities will never define me and give hope to the next generation. Although, I'd never thought that I would see this unfold right in front of me. To give at least one person hope? That's all I could have wished for.

Today, I am going to give my final speech as head girl to the year group; to say I am nervous would be an understatement. I have been thinking about what I wanted to say for weeks. I hope this will be something that the rest of the year group will take with them; if not, it might be a funny video on YouTube.

I walk into the main hall with the rest of my tutor and sit in my normal seat with my cue cards firmly tucked into my top blazer pocket. My palms are sweaty, and I notice that I am constantly playing with my hair. I check that I don't have a boogie hanging out of my nose or that my makeup is perfect in my Minnie Mouse pocket mirror so many times that Josie takes it off me.

As usual, Mr Perkins waits for all of us to be seated before he makes his way up to the main podium. "Good afternoon. I can definitely feel a lot of excitement in the room."

There are a couple of cheers and claps.

"Well, what can I say about this year group? Being your Head of Year for the last seven years has been an absolute honour. Yes, it hasn't always been plain sailing, to say the least."

There are a few laughs from those who had maybe made his role challenging at times.

"I wouldn't want it any other way as you've all now become strong, independent individuals who are more than ready for the outside world. I think I speak for the rest of the teaching team that we wish each and every one of you the best of luck with your future endeavours. I can remember having my last assembly when I was your age. Before you say it, yes, it was a long time ago!"

This sends the year group into fits of laughter.

He continues, "However, I never thought back then that my job would be to watch young adults flourish and support them to find their passions in life. So, with that, I would like to introduce someone who has shown that even when life throws us obstacles or challenges, we can overcome them in order to succeed. It's my pleasure and honour to welcome your head girl, Miss Amy Webb."

The whole year group stands up and cheers as I make my way up to the front.

The applause fills the entirety of the hall. I take a deep breath when I reach the podium and place my cue cards by the microphone. "Good afternoon, I can't tell you how nervous I am about making this speech, but I'll give it a go!

"When I think back to our first day of Year 7, we were all completely different people as to who we are now. We have gained knowledge, confidence, and skills that we can take into our next stage of life. The thing that I wasn't expecting to learn was courage. As I know you're all aware, life hasn't always been easy for me, but I try to think about what I have achieved, which makes me extremely proud. Unfortunately for teenagers and young adults, society puts us into boxes, whether you're the sporty one or the one that's good at maths. Doing this can make teenagers and young adults feel constrictive and sometimes worthless. We all have strengths, and they should be celebrated more often. Take Josie, for instance, her sewing skills are terrible and should never be trusted anywhere near a sewing machine but asked her to chat up anyone, and she's your girl."

Everyone applauds and laughs at this.

"If I stayed in my box of having cerebral palsy and epilepsy, then I might not have been at this school, and I certainly wouldn't have been appointed head girl. The word disability is defined as any condition of the body or mind, also known as an impairment, that makes it more difficult for the person to do certain activities. If that's the case, then don't we all have a disability? As humans, we all have difficulties that we face in our lives; we should all celebrate our uniqueness. I found that throughout being in education, individuals who have additional needs are, for some reason, outcasts. It's as though we are thought as being unable to achieve anything simply because we have a condition that we didn't actually ask for in the first place. I know I've been incredibly lucky to be surrounded by people who only see me for me. Emma, Josie, you've never asked me to be something I'm not, but you definitely take advantage of the perks that come with having a disability. Jack you've always there through the ups and downs and for that I'm so grateful.

"It's so crucial that, we should never judge others on their abilities or disabilities because you have no idea what it's like to be them. We are who we are, and we should never feel discouraged by this. My disabilities have never and will never define me. It's our responsibility as humans to make sure that we treat anybody and everybody with the respect and dignity we would want to receive ourselves.

"It has been my privilege and honour to be your head girl and something that I will never forget. It's now up to us to go against tradition and reach the potential we are all capable of. So, with that in mind, and my last duty as head girl, it's my pleasure to announce a new award that will be given out every year, which with the help of Mr Perkins, we have named it the Inspirational Student Award. The award will be given to students who have shown immense levels of courage and defied expectations to achieve great things. I want to thank Mr Perkins and the senior leadership team for awarding me with this position and hope that I've made you proud. Finally, I would like to end with a quote that inspires me. Reach for the moon; even if you fall short, you will land among the stars. Congratulations, Year 13, we did it!"

I look up from my cue cards and am faced with a sea of students standing up, clapping, and whistling. Everything has slowed down. I can really saviour this moment. I turn to my left as Mr Perkins comes towards me with the biggest smile I have ever seen.

He shakes my hand and whispers, "I cannot tell you how proud I am of you right now."

After a few moments, the noise dies down, and I make my way back to my seat.

"Well, I don't really know how to top that. Amy, everything you've overcome and achieved is amazing. You're such an inspiration to others who think they can't do it. Now I realise that we normally have a head boy speech as well. However, as I said before, we thought we should change and mix things up, with that speech I'm pleased we decided to changed tradition."

The whole of the year group turned towards Josh to see his reaction. He looks a little relieved. Josh may be high achieving but having worked with him closely this year, I've realised that he sometimes lacks confidence. Finally, we are free.

After the assembly, we sign each other's shirts and write

messages in each of our yearbooks. I put several photos in mine from over the years, which bring back so many unforgettable memories. Just like that, we are done! I feel a mixture of emotions, a sense of freedom, and a sense of panic because I am not entirely sure what the next phase of my life will be.

chapter 19

The biggest night of the year is only a few days away. I need to go into school to finish off some things before saying my final goodbyes to a place that has taught me so much. Josie, Emma, and I decide to go into together as we have basically been inseparable since our last exam. Whilst I am there, I pop into Mr Perkin's office. Even though we didn't always see eye to eye this year, he has given me a fantastic opportunity and saw something in me that not many have previously. I know that many teachers were very anxious about whether or not I would make a suitable head girl, but I'm so glad that Mr Perkins has never had any of those doubts. "Mr Perkins, have you got a minute?"

He stands up from his desk and gestures for me to take my usual seat. "Amy, of course, please do come in and take a seat. I can't believe that we've nearly reached the end of the year."

He looked like he is about to tear up. "You know what, Amy, when we appointed you as our head girl, we did it because we knew you would bring determination to the role and show younger years that anyone can do anything if they put their mind to it. Amy, you're such a role model. I know so many students look up to you because you show them that anything is possible without a lot of hard work and determination. The resilience that you've shown this year to keep going has been phenomenal. You're a student that teachers certainly won't forget. I'm not sure how you've been so positive all year. If I was in your position I definitely would have crumbled."

I hope he means this in a good way.

"Also, I must say that your speech was so inspiring; I just wish that all of the students at the school got to hear. Have you thought about a career in public speaking?"

For the first time in a long time, I'm overwhelmed with pride and joy. I've been able to make a difference to this school. "Sir, I would like to add something."

"Anything."

I clear my throat and take a moment to work out how I'm going to word this so that it comes out correctly.

"I want to see teachers and support staff at this school undergo more training about inclusion and diversity. What happened with Miss Stevens, and I shouldn't have happened. I feel there's still a stigma around disability. Attitudes need to change, and people need to be educated. I don't have a choice about my disability, but we all have choice to accept individuals with disabilities no matter what they are within society."

Mr Perkins bows his head. "I completely understand what you mean, and I'm blown away. Even on your final day, where you have every right to be a bit selfish, you're still fighting hard for change. I *can* assure you; there have been many conversations within staff meetings about inclusion and diversity. I think one of the main problems is that when we were your age these topics weren't really spoken about. Disability was a subject that many people would and still do shy away from. We as a school need to change how we view and approach these subjects because, honestly, I think some teachers are too scared to ask the questions that would then trigger conversations."

Finally, it feels like I'm being heard. "Exactly, sir. As I've always said, I would much rather someone ask about my disabilities than make assumptions on what I can and can't do. My mum has always said that I haven't stopped fighting for change since the doctors cut my umbilical cord. You know confidence hasn't ever been an issue for me; I'm sure it never will be."

He chuckles at this. "I'm happy to answer any questions that staff, teachers or even parents have. This will not change unless we talk about it. For too many years, individuals with disabilities, either visible or non-visible, have been made to feel outcast. Like they only belong with people who are just like them. We should celebrate our differences instead of causing them to divide us. I feel this country has come a long way with acceptance and allowing individuals into society who have disabilities, but there's still a long way to go. We now have a duty to make sure that voices are being heard, opinions are shared and respected. This will then hopefully lead to change.

"Amy, the power and determination you show when you talk is inspiring. What's so unique is that you also have the knowledge to back your points up. You know exactly what you're talking about, and I know with you'll go far. I'm certain that this is only the beginning of your journey; I can't wait to see what you come up with next. Anyway, Amy, what was it that you popped in for?"

I almost forgot my original reason why I came into his office.

"Oh yes, sorry, sir. Well, I know it's a tradition for the head boy and head girl to travel to prom in the same car." I can tell that he was nervous as to what I was about to say.

"Well, I don't want to get you involved in teenage drama, but let's just say that there has been a lot between Josh and I." He laughs but doesn't comment on this statement. I forge ahead,

"So, with that in mind, I was wondering if I could travel to prom with my friends instead?"

Mr Perkins inhales rather loudly. "I'm sorry, Amy, but that's tradition. This one is out of my control. For nearly thirty years now, the head boy and the head girl have always travelled to the prom together."

I was disappointed and was almost eager to fight back; however, after all the school has done for me this year, it is probably the least I could do for them.

"You've definitely changed many traditions this year for the better, so with that in mind, why don't we take out the first dance?" he says.

I almost completely blanked out this part of the prom, and for a good reason, I'm a terrible dancer and the thought of the whole year group watching me dance makes me sick to my stomach.

"Ok, deal." I shake Mr Perkins hand and then let myself out of the office. It's weird leaving school in the middle of the day, but I am not going to complain about being able to go home and not having the stresses of revision or coursework to do.

The following day, Mum and I go and pick up my prom dress. I need to have it altered as the skirt part was too long, and it would have caught on my frame. As I walk into the shop, I notice rails of dresses of in every colour of the rainbow. They also cater for weddings; I start to get very excited as I think about one day marrying the man of my dreams.

"May I help you?" A lady that only looks a few years older than me is standing by one of the rails.

"Hi, yeah, I've come to collect a dress."

She looks ready to type in my name to the computer. "And what was the name, please?"

"It's Amy Webb."

She types it in and smiles back at me. "Oh yes, let me go and get that for you. Would you like to try it on here?"

I'm unsure whether the changing rooms are accessible.

"How big are your changing rooms?" I hate asking this, but I need to ensure that there's enough room and didn't want Mum paying for something that might not fit.

She smiles. "We have a larger changing room at the end. You're more than welcome to use this if you would like?"

She ushers me through to the changing room, and after inspecting it, I'm satisfied with the space. The shop assistant helps me into my dress whilst Mum wait on the comfy sofa. Before I open the curtain, I take a minute to look in the mirror. For once, I feel like an actual princess instead of the girl with cerebral palsy. The dress is beautiful; it's a dark blue colour with Demonte's covering it, with an underskirt to make it swish whilst dancing and a sweetheart neckline. The shop made sure that they took it up enough so that it wouldn't get caught in my wheels or the possibility of stepping on it.

The minute the shop assistant pulls open the curtain, Mum starts to sob.

"Oh, darling, you look absolutely stunning."

I can barely understand her through all the tears; sometimes, she can be so embarrassing. I dread to think what she will be like if I ever try on a wedding dress. I know this was the only time she will see her one and only daughter in a prom dress about to finish school, so it's a big moment for her.

The shop assistant puffs out the bottom of the dress to show the full effect and asks while looking at me through the mirror. "So, are you happy?"

Mum reaches for a tissue as she has mascara lines down her face.

I smile. "Very, thank you for all your help."

After a while of staring at myself in the mirror, I decide to get change back into my regular clothes, which I don't feel like a princess in. Mum is still in tears, and she gets her purse out of her bag to pay for my dress. Mum also buys me a small silver bag with a chain to hook onto my frame.

"It's my pleasure Amy. I hope you have an amazing night!" The shop assistant puts my dress in one of those bags that you get from the dry cleaner's.

Mum picks it up from the counter and holds the door open for me.

I have to rest for the remainder of the time before prom as it is going to be such a busy night. It isn't all bad, though, as I can get away with watching *Scrubs* reruns till my heart is content. I am doubly excited as Josie is throwing an after-prom party as well; I just hope it goes better than the Halloween party. After working so hard for the last month to get everything done, I definitely deserve a night to let my hair down. Josie has warned me that she had invited Jack, although I didn't mind, we've got to move past this and be comfortable being in the same room as each other. The only downside to prom is that I have to travel with Josh, which I know will be so awkward.

chapter 20

Worrying about what I would like for prom is exhausting. Physically and mentally, I've done so many practice runs of my makeup I can almost do it in my sleep. Mum booked a hairdresser to come to our house this afternoon to make me look somewhat presentable, hopefully. I made sure that I saved some money from Christmas to go to one of those big department stores with all the makeup counters. I purchase my first MAC lipstick in Syrup which is purple/neutral shade as the last thing I want is bright lipstick smudged all over my face. Mum had found some cute little silver flat pumps that would go with my dress. Emma and Josie arrive so that we can all get ready together. Mum also gets out our fancy glasses and opens a bottle of wine. We very rarely actually use them, so Mum has to scrap off the thick layer of dust on them.

"A toast?" Mum holds her glass up in the air. "I'm so proud of all of you. From being kids that would always steal my makeup so often that I had to lock it in a draw to now being three independent, strong women with such a bright future ahead of you. I know that you will excel at whatever you ladies touch, but make sure you mention me in your memoir. Please stop growing up; you're making me feel so old! I remember my own end of year ball, unsure what I was going to do with my life. I'm still unsure even at forty, but one thing that I am proud of is raising an inspirational and independent daughter."

Mum is in tears whilst raising her glass to clink with us. Mum's speech is uplifting; I love how she's not only supported me but also the people that mean the world to me. I can't help but worry that I have no backup for next year whilst I'm waiting to reaudition. For someone who always likes to have a plan for everything, this really isn't helpful.

The hairdresser arrives. She is happy to do Josie's and Emma's hair as well, which I think is strange. Obviously, this is something that Mum had also organised. My bedroom is being used for us to get into our dresses after we have done our makeup.

Josie is having her hair done whilst Emma and I sit on the sofa.

"So, how do you feel about tonight, Amy?" Josie asks.

Since I told Jack about what happened between Josh and I, he hasn't spoken to me at all, which I can completely understand. I'm still gutted about what happened with his ex as well; the thought of the two of them makes me feel sick.

"I feel alright, I mean, this is sort of the end of my role, which I'm so honoured to have done, but I'm looking forward to the next chapter, whatever that may be." I know that wasn't what Josie was referring to but don't want to bring it up as this is our prom night.

"Amy, I'm just going to ask you straight up. Can you see anything happening between you and Josh?" she asks.

I've been thinking a lot about this week.

"Honestly, no, he's such a nice guy, and that kiss was amazing, but . . ." I can't say it.

"He's not Jack." I'm so glad Emma finished it off for me.

With an hour to go until Josh is here to pick me up, I need to get into my dress. Getting into dresses isn't exactly easy for me, but Mum and I have devised a method over the years. I sit on my bed and get one leg in at a time whilst holding onto my frame and then stand up but have my frame facing the wrong way so that I can use all three sides to hold onto.

Once I get the dress up to my waist, Mum then finds the armholes and holds them up to my chest. I then let go of my frame one arm at a time and then finally stand up while Mum zips up the back. I stand in front of the full-length mirror. I can't immediately pick out anything wrong with me. For once, all I could see in the reflection staring back at me is Amy. Not the girl who uses a walking frame or has seizures. Not the girl with hands that can look awkward or legs that have big, chunky splits to keep them in place. I just see eighteen-year-old me with my whole future ahead of me.

"You look stunning, Amy." Mum kisses me on the cheek as she's standing behind me. She then helps me with the final touches and put on a necklace that once belonged to my grandma. Even though I've don't remember her, as she passed away when I was a baby, Mum always tells me how proud she would be of me.

"Amy, you ready? I don't think I've ever been prouder of you. This is the end of your journey in education, but I know this is just the start of your story. The world needs to hear your story because I think you could make a real impact and give hope to people who are in similar positions to you."

I am trying my hardest not to cry, ruining my makeup would've been a disaster!

"Come on," she says. "Josh will be here in a minute."

Just as I am about to walk into the living room, Emma stops me. "No, wait there, Josh needs to know how way out of his league you really are!" She winks.

Josie and Emma are also in their dresses. I know I have beautiful friends, but tonight they both look drop-dead gorgeous. Josie's dress is ruby red, off the shoulder and has the most exquisite rose flowers details covering the top half of the dress. It looks more like she is going to a film premiere.

Emma's dress is a bit more simple, royal blue full-length halter neck. She pairs it with silver stilettos heals and looks amazing. Mum gets out her phone and takes photos of us three together. Josie suggests that she take one of Mum and me, and here come the waterworks once again.

"Well, ladies, you both looked stunning," Josh says.

I can hear the three of them having this conversation whilst I was still in the kitchen. "I suppose there's only one person missing. Where's our head girl?"

This is my cue to make a grand entrance. Josh looks so handsome, rocking a black suit with a matching bow tie.

"Wow, I must be one lucky chap. Amy, you look absolutely stunning." He walks over and kisses me on the cheek.

Josie and Emma's car arrive shortly after that; Josie's dad paid for them to go in an Aston Martin convertible. The driver is dressed in a suit like a proper chauffeur and makes sure that both their doors are open before they even walk out of the front door.

As I am looking out the window, a gorgeous black Rolls Royce pulls up on the drive. The driver ensures that I am safely in the car before putting my frame in the boot. I've never worn a dress this elegant; I am nervous about getting some of it caught in the door. The doors open the other way to an average car which is easier for me to get in, but somehow, I can't see Mum buying one of these anytime soon. Mum and some of the neighbours are standing by the car, taking photos, wishing that we had a fantastic time. It is strange how much our reputation has changed over this past year, but there is no way that I am going to complain about the attention.

I am nervous about what we were going to talk about for the twenty-minute car journey to school. Josh looks out of the window for the first part of the journey, nothing like an awkward silence. "So, Amy, before we get to prom, I need to address something."

"Yes?"

He clears his throat. "I need to know where your head is at regarding us?"

"Look, Josh, you're a really great guy, and I know you're going to go on to do amazing things. I understand that we had our moments where my head has gone there, and I've thought about whether we could be more. However, I'm sorry, I just think that we are about to go on completely different life paths, and I couldn't see it." I feel awful letting him down on the way to prom; what a way to bruise a guy's ego. Unfortunately, it has to be done.

"Well, thank you for being honest. Friends? Also, I can see how happy he makes you." He holds his hand out for me to shake it. I am a little confused about the comment but just brush over it.

"Deal." I shake.

"Pleasure doing business with you, Miss Webb."

I laugh; he can be so quirky sometimes.

It's bizarre driving past the bus stop and going through

the main gates that are usually closed.

The noise that we could hear from inside the car makes it like we are at a film premiere with all the paparazzi trying to get a photo.

Both the doors are opened, and standing behind mine is Mr Perkins. "Wow, Amy, you look lovely."

I can hear the ear-splitting noise of two hundred pupils and teachers. All I can see are people in every colour of the rainbow.

I know I need to concentrate on getting out of the car, as it could ended in disaster. What if my dress gets caught? What if someone moves my frame as I'm leaning on it to get out of the car and land flat on my face? Well, that's one way to go viral, I suppose.

The driver somehow manages to get around to the boot, retrieve my frame, and then places it by my door before I notice that he has even gotten out of the car. Thankfully I can see Josie and Emma at the front of the crowd. As we make our way up to the main doors to the school, everyone else follows behind us. We are then given the honours to open the even for the year group by cutting the ribbon attach to the main doors of the school.

All of us gather in the main hall for pre-drinks as if we are at a wedding. Proms that have been held previous years would begin with the head boy and girl having their first dance whilst everyone else gathers in a large circle around them. I'm so glad that we went for a night at the movies theme. The design team has done an amazing job with film reels, black and white clapper board signs everywhere and even a red carpet.

Mr Perkins wanted me to keep our deal a secret from everyone else apart from Josh. Thankfully he is fine with it and confessed that he was a terrible dancer. Together we decide to have the first song as S-Clubs 7's "Reach."

Emma, Josie, and I are taking several photos throughout the night. We even take one with Mr Perkins. Surprisingly, he seemed more than up for it. We are also able to put a marquee outside of the foyer to have somewhere that students could go for a breather. After fighting through the crowd, Josie and I manage to find an empty table whilst Emma goes to get us some drinks. Josie is scanning the room, probably seeing who she could go home with; seriously, I can't take her anywhere. Due to her detective skills, she always knows who has just broken up and even who's about to find out that they've been cheated on.

"Right as both my girls are here; I've got something I need to tell you. I've known this quite a while but didn't want to tell you and then get my hopes up. I received an offer from Oxford University to study psychology." Immediately Emma jumps into both our arms, as I'm sure saying it made it feel more real.

"Why didn't you tell us you were even applying?" I ask.

"Amy, I don't know if you're aware, but I'm not exactly the smartest girl. I thought even making the application felt like a bit of a joke, which is why I didn't tell you."

"I'm so proud of you, Emma. You're going to smash this! Right, let's get onto the bigger news. Have you spoken to Jack yet?" She's immediately expecting an answer.

"No, and I don't know if I'm going to; after all, this is his prom too. I just feel that it would be better if we did it somewhere else. I'm sure I'll see him soon."

They both look at each other like they definitely aren't expecting that kind of response.

"Amy, what are you talking about? You and Jack are meant to be together. You two just need to get over yourselves and realise this." Same old Emma, telling it exactly as it is. "Look, you and Josh are nothing, and after tonight you won't probably see or possibly even speak to each other. I could see how happy Jack made you, and you two just click. I know you don't want to admit it because you're so bloody stubborn, but you and Jack just work."

She's right yet again.

"I know, I know, but what if we do go back there and it doesn't work out again? It's just going to cause more damage to our friendship."

Emma suddenly drops her head. "Let me spell it out for you. You two broke up because you both had so much going on, and it was better to be apart, right?"

"Yeah?"

"Well, in case you weren't aware, this is our prom, after tonight, you're free."

Still, I don't know if I had the guts to have that conversation with him.

She says, "Look, I can tell you're nervous, but you won't know until you try." And with that she gives me a gentle nudge.

Jack is in the corner of the main hall with a few of his mates, making me even more nervous. I stop and take out my phone to try and text him to come over. Still, just as I am typing the text, Emma says, "NO, you need to do this in person. Go!"

Thankfully, just before I reach the group, Jack sees me and excuses himself. "Hey, drink?"

I nod and smile. He goes in front of me. Indiscreetly both Josie and Emma stare and he says, "Alright, ladies looking lovely. I'll see you in a bit."

We make our way out of the main hall and through to the marquee, which thankfully is a lot quieter than earlier. I sit down at one of the tables at the back of the marquees whilst Jack gets us both a can of Coke from the makeshift bar.

"Thanks, so are you having a good night?" I ask, feeling more like I've just met him in a bar rather than talking to my best friend.

"Look, I realise that I never apologised for the way that I acted when I heard about you and Josh. I'm actually really happy for you both," he says.

"Well, thanks, but nothing actually happened between

us. I even told him on the way here that nothing is going to happen between us."

"You let someone down on the way to prom! Way to bruise a guy's ego, Amy! I can't say that I wasn't hurt to hear that you were going out for ice cream with someone that I still can't stand, but I understand why you did what you did."

"I'm so sorry for hurting you. That's the last thing I wanted to do. Even though I haven't fully forgiven for what you did with Beth, I do understand. We all make mistakes. You've forgiven me, so I guess it's right to do the same for you as well. I still care about you a lot."

He has that cheeky little smile that I've missed so much. "Care about or love?"

I'm stunned that he has the guts to ask this because even though he appears to be cocky most of the time, there is still definitely a shy side to him.

"Don't push it. Can we just go back to how we were?"

He looks back at me.

"No." His voice is cold as if I hit a nerve.

This is a disaster; I just wish I could go back and not kiss Josh because then I wouldn't be in this mess.

"No, because why would I settle for you being my best friend when I still love you and always will."

I'm absolutely gobsmacked that these words had come out of his mouth. Before I can string a sentence together, his lips are on mine. I don't care that other people are around us because every time I kiss him, it feels like we are the only two people in the world, and nothing else matters.

I look up at him whilst still being in his arms.

"You know I still love you, right?" He presses his nose against mine.

"I do now."

In perfect timing, the deejay starts "Never Gonna Let You Down" by Colbie Caillat, which is a song that I associate so much with him. I feel so safe with Jack.

"Come on, let's go dance!" he says and before I can say no, I am already in the middle of the dance floor dancing to one of my favourite songs. Just like that, those butterflies come back into my stomach, and somehow, they feel more potent this time. Thankfully Josie and Emma tag along too; I'm sure they just wanted to witness what was going to happen next.

I press my lips on his. "You're the best thing that happened to me, and I never want you to forget that."

He smiles back at me. "I never thought that I could fall in love at eighteen, but you, Amy, have made that happen, just promise me something?" I am suspicious as to what he is going to say next. "Never stopped loving me."

"I promise, why would I give up something as amazing as this? I love you so much and I never want to let you go again." The same feeling I had on New Year's Eve comes rushing back.

The rest of the night is a bit of a blur. All I remember is smiling a lot.

chapter 21

Somehow, I manage to make it home. As I stretch to wake up, I notice Jack is fast asleep next to me on the floor. "Why aren't you at home?" He jumps so much; he must have been in a real deep sleep.

"Well, Mum knew that you didn't have a lift to get home, so we drove you home. I then wanted to make sure that you had your medication as your mum was asleep by the time we got back here, so I just crashed on the floor as I didn't want Mum waiting for me." Somehow, even when he's half asleep, he's still way too good for me.

"I hope the floor wasn't too hard for you?"

He smiles.

"I'm used to having hard things." He pokes his tongue out at me.

I duck my head down under my duvet, trying not to

laugh.

"Oh, come on, I can show you if you like," he says whilst winking at me and sticking out his tongue. He leaps onto the bed and tickles me until I let out a big squeak.

"How did we get back here?" I'm trying to work out what happened last night for us to wake up together.

"Well, like I just said, I want to make sure you were safe. Come on, Amy, I know you've got brain damage, but it can't be that bad." He is avoiding the question that I am actually asking.

"No, you know what I mean."

"I do, but it's always fun winding you up, I don't know. I guess when you fall in love with someone that never really goes away. I meant what I said last night. I love you and am going to be here for the good bits and the rubbish bits as well." He leans over to kiss me. "I'll go and make us some breakfast."

"Breakfast in bed; you really can be a gentleman."

Jack peers back around the door. "Yeah, don't get used to it." He displays that cheeky smile that I adore.

"Good morning, Jack!"

Oh no! I didn't realise Mum would be up already. I really want to hear what they were saying in the kitchen. I just scroll through my phone because I can't wait to see all the photos posted last night. Since I can't really remember the after party given that I was so tired, it will be nice to see what actually happened. As I was trying to piece the events of last night together, Josie texts.

"WHAT A PARTY! I heard you, and Jack left together. GET IN THEIR GIRL! XX."

Clearly, we also hooked up at the after-party, that's one of the problems of having epilepsy is when I'm super tired, it's almost like I'm drunk.

"What actually happened? XX"

All I can remember right now is kissing Jack at prom, and then somehow, I wake up to him on my floor.

"Well, I wasn't actually there when it happened, but from what you told me, you and Jack went out to the bar area and then when you came back, you were all over each other. I'm so happy for you, hun xx."

Now it's starting to come back to me; I remember sitting with Jack, and then somehow we ended up kissing, but how we got there I'm still unsure of.

"Are you happy? Xx"

I think she might have thought that Jack and I hooking up was a mistake, but it definitely wasn't. After all, the feelings are still there. Jack climbs back into bed and snuggles into me, the best feeling in the world.

"So, do you want to talk about last night?" I need to know whether last night a mistake for him or he actually meant what he said.

"Amy, do we really need to?"

Oh no, this was a mistake. Stay calm, he's broken my heart once, and he's about to do it again.

I remain silent as I try to hold back the tears.

"Amy, I broke up with you because,".

I cut him off. "I thought you said it wasn't a breakup; it was a break?"

I can tell that all Jack wanted to do was kiss me, but I am having none of it.

"Amy, I thought I needed to be on my own to figure my life out. After doing this for only a few weeks, I've realised that my life is already figured out and do you want to know why?"

I shake my head.

"It's because I have you in my life. Amy, you make my life so much better; you bring me so much joy. Your positive outlook on your life is inspiring, and I know, whatever happens, you're going to be successful because you've already worked so hard to get to where you are. One thing I can promise you, and this time I mean it, whatever happens, we will do it together."

"So, what you're saying is you can't live without me."

"Well, I've realised that if I'm going to do my law degree, I'm going to need my greatest supporter. Oh, yeah, did I not tell you I've got my place at West Brooklyn Law School. So yes, Cinderella, your Prince Charming is here to rescue you and sweep you off your feet." He picks me up from the bed and throws me in the air.

"Wait, what?" I laugh. "You're going to law school? Baby, I'm so proud of you. I'm so proud that you finally realised that you're an incredible person and you're going to make an amazing lawyer."

"That's right, beautiful, you've shown me that I'm smarter than I think, and why should I also reach for my dreams."

I'm so proud of him for finally realising after all these years that anything is possible.

A little while after breakfast, my phone buzzes from a number that I didn't know.

"Hello?" My voice sounds croaky as I hadn't really spoken enough, and I was shouting a lot of last night.

"Good morning. Is that Amy?"

Now I am even more confused.

"Speaking."

"Hello, there, my name is Heidi, and I'm calling from the council."

Immediately, I tensed up. I'm sure it's something to do with my Personal Independence Payments.

"Just so you know, there's nothing to worry about."

I'm sure she could sense that I was worried as I wasn't saying anything.

"I was calling you as I'm one of the inclusion officers for education." This information makes me even more confused.

"We have heard what you've been doing at your school as head girl and have heard from your head of year, Mr Perkins, what amazing changes you've made in under a year. Mr Perkins has told us about your determination and how you don't take no for an answer. So, with that in mind, we were wondering if you would be interested in joining our team as an inclusion officer apprentice? We think you're so inspiring by how you've overcome so much and are now such a role model. Amy, I wish there were more people like you to inspire others."

I am in a state of shock. How have I, someone who has literally just finished school, been offered a job? "Um, I'm not going to lie to you. I'm baffled right now. I don't have any experience, though."

Heidi chuckles. "Amy, with your story and everything you've been through, that is the best experience you could need. Everything that you could possibly need to inspire others you already have within you. We just want to provide an outlet for you to use that experience for good."

Hearing this makes me smile uncontrollably because for so long I've felt like my disability was a burden. "Wow! Well, thank you, I would be overjoyed to join your team. Thank you so much. My disability has never been used in such a positive way, so for you to say all those amazing things really has caught me off guard."

"Brilliant! I will send over your job offer in an email, and we look forward to you starting with us soon. Congratulations Amy!"

I put down my phone and looked straight at Jack; I'm sure he could sense this wasn't like the RADA call.

"Babe, I've just been offered a job." I'm unsure what else

to say as I am still in shock.

He scoops me up from the bed and gives me the biggest kiss. " OH, MY GOODNESS! I'm so proud of you, baby. Wait, what's the job?"

How do I even explain this to him? "Well, I think I'm going to be an inclusion officer apprentice, but I'm not sure why."

"Babe, are you kidding? This job is perfect for you. You haven't seen how passionate you look when you talk about disabilities. Now you have an amazing opportunity to make a difference to those who need you most. Come on, text the girls." Jack suddenly whips me up into his arms and carries me into the living room.

"What's going on? Amy, are your legs, ok?" Mum always goes straight to the worst scenario.

"So . . ." I'm trying to compose myself; I can't believe that this was real. "I've just had a phone call from the inclusion team at the council."

I may not be going to drama school, but I do still love to give a bit of suspense.

"Oh, come on, Amy, this is killing me!"

I decide it's best I put her out of her misery.

"I've just had a phone call from the inclusion team at the council. I've been offered a position as an inclusion officer apprentice. Finally, I can get my voice heard and support those who need it most."

"OH, MY GOODNESS AMY! I'm so proud of you."

As usual, here come the waterworks. I think Mum has cried more than I have this year.

Even though RADA has been my dream for so long and making it big on the West End, I know this was going to be the safer option. If being head girl has taught me anything, it's that I've got the confidence to tell my story so that hopefully it can inspire and support others to reach their full potential.

"You know what I've just realised is, sometimes it's good to have dreams and aspirations even if they seem almost impossible. However, what's even more important is looking at what we already have, who we are and what's important to us. Being head girl, this year has been such an amazing opportunity and not just to voice my opinion but also to see that my disability can be a positive thing. It's crucial that we use these values as seeds to grow into our lives' passions. I'm so lucky that I'm able to have an opinion and voice it because so many people don't.

I wanted to go into the acting business to see my name in bright lights on the West End but also to make the sector more inclusive. Now I can make changes to a broader audience, plus I don't have to go through the gruelling experiences of going to auditions and rejections.

Mum is still tearing up. "Amy, you've shown strength in the toughest of moments. You show every day that it's ok to be proud to be who you are. I feel so honoured to call you my daughter, and honestly, I don't think you would have this passion and drive if you weren't disabled."

If you told me back in September that this was how my final year would pan out, I wouldn't have believed you because it's been one that I'll never forget. I guess it's true what they say life is what you make it!

Printed in Great Britain
by Amazon

81606021R00153